Ivywood Manor

THE DRIFTLESS UNSOLICITED NOVELLA SERIES

Ivywood Manor
A GOTHIC NOVELLA
by Tani Loo

BRAIN MILL PRESS

GREEN BAY, WISCONSIN

Published in the United States by Brain Mill Press.

Print ISBN 978-1-948559-41-6

EPUB ISBN 978-1-948559-44-7

MOBI ISBN 978-1-948559-42-3

PDF ISBN 978-1-948559-43-0

Cover art by Rovina Cai.

www.brainmillpress.com

Published by Brain Mill Press, the Driftless Unsolicited Novella Series publishes those novellas selected as winners of the Driftless Unsolicited Novella Contest each year.

For my parents, Garry and Sherrie

Ivywood Manor

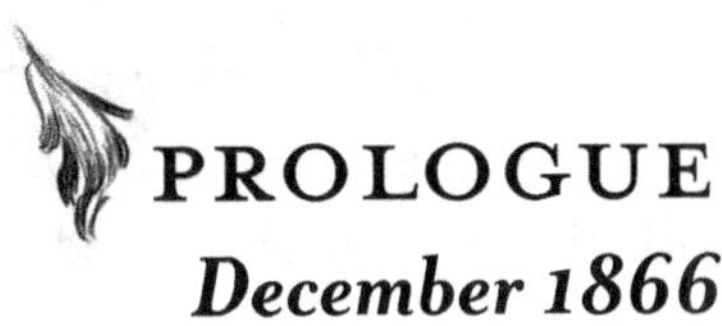

PROLOGUE
December 1866

I WAS NINE WHEN THE MAN FETCHED ME FROM THE ORPHANAGE AS THE SUN ROSE, BURNT ORANGE TURNING CERULEAN BEFORE MY EYES. He was thin, and his head was topped with a mop of dark hair. When he flashed a smile at me, his skin looked as if it were being stretched too tight. His pupils were toffee and his eyebrows thick, but his voice was smooth, silky almost. The sounds emitted reminded me of warm milk sliding down my throat.

Nancy, the plump woman in charge, dragged me out of bed and coaxed me into the garments the orphanage provided. It was the first time I'd seen the stained white dress and matching bonnet, and both items were constricting. But Nancy paid no mind as she urged me to stand closer to the man, even closer as we neared the front door.

Outside, drops of water from the rooftop splattered upon my head. It must've rained the night before. The man was holding a stack of adoption papers, and he shifted it beneath his armpit the way that I unstuck horehound candy from the roof of my mouth and slid it beneath my tongue; he kept it hidden from the sun's rays.

"She has no possessions?" the man inquired.

"None," Nancy confirmed. "Her mother told us the girl's name before she passed, but that's all she managed to do."

Though I watched Nancy carefully as she spoke, I detected no sign of sympathy from her. My mother's death was simply another one laid on the orphanage's doorstep. The man, on the other hand, shifted uncomfortably.

"Charlotte Herring," he murmured, glancing at me. "Yes, my solicitor has arranged for her to keep her name in the paperwork. You will see it has been sorted out."

Nancy narrowed her eyes. "If you don't mind me saying, sir, it's mighty unusual to let the girl keep the name Herring. I understand that you'd rather she didn't take yours, but most like to cut ties to the family."

The man's smile was tight. "This adoption is unusual in itself, is it not?"

Nancy's face fell momentarily, as if she were concerned that the man would no longer take me. Then she pasted a wide grin on her face. "Unusual perhaps, but a decision you won't regret."

The man nodded, proffering his hand to me.

I hesitated, so he introduced himself to me. He

called himself Morton van Kirk, told me of an estate called Ivywood Manor, and pointed his finger toward an open carriage door. In response, I stared at the mud on my slippers, dirtied by the brown water running down the street. I didn't know this man with the sweet words dripping from the corners of his mouth.

But when I glanced back at Nancy, I realized that nothing waited for me there. I accepted his help into the carriage but not his hand. He wasn't shaken by the way I ignored his kindness, and I thought better of him for it.

When we arrived at Ivywood Manor, Mr. van Kirk helped me exit the carriage. We traversed the last few feet of the path on foot, my toes rolling over pieces of gravel like they were marbles, before he stopped and knelt in his spotless pants. He reached for my hands to press them between his own, and I was shocked by the heat emanating from him. I shivered.

The corner of his lip curved upward, sympathetic. "Now then, I know this journey has been taxing for you, but we have finally arrived. We are going to enter Ivywood now. Ivywood will be your home, and if you ever want for anything, you come to me."

I didn't know what to say, so I nodded.

He extended his hand and patted me on the head—a gesture that I found oddly comforting. Then he straightened and revealed his open palm for me to place my hand within his. I stared at it, nearly even grabbed it, when I realized we were being watched.

A boy with dark hair and brown flecks in his eyes stood opposite us. He stared at me through the wrought iron gates with his face pressed against the bars. His eyebrows were thick and umber like the hair on his head, but his lips were almost puce.

"Father," the boy said.

"Victor, open the gate, will you?"

The boy, Victor, inclined his head, but his eyes never left mine. His gaze was so open, so grave, that I began to imagine the flecks in his eyes were changing colors. Were they really brown? Or were they black? Was it the sunlight hitting them that made it seem so? He continued to stare at me, but I found no answer.

Victor took a step backward and opened the gates.

"Victor is my son," Mr. van Kirk informed me. "You are only a year apart in age. He is younger, yet I trust you will get along well."

"Yes," I said. "Of course."

Mr. van Kirk led me past the gates, pausing to place a firm hand of acknowledgment on Victor's shoulder. The gesture bunched up Victor's fitted suit. He inclined his head toward me.

I jumped, nearly forgetting that I should curtsy back.

The manor reminded me of a church in Ascot, except the manor's walls were made of brick instead of stone and the grounds stretched twice as far and wide. Instead of other buildings on its sides, the manor had trees with branches extending so tall that I wondered if they could touch the clouds. I couldn't imagine that I'd live in this castle. Nancy hadn't even allowed me inside the church; she'd said I came from the womb of a woman who knew too many gods, though she'd tell me no more than that.

Water spilled over the edges of a large, ornate fountain in the center of the grounds. It accumulated into one slate gray pool, then the next. On its sides were dirt-covered remnants of a garden. I memorized the way the few brittle stems drooped and tangled with one another, so that I could look up whether the flowers could be salvaged later.

Mr. van Kirk called to us both in his silky voice, and we continued toward the manor. That's when I noticed the ravens: gnarled stone carvings piled upon blocks until they were equal in height to the door's entrance. Every angry, minute detail was carved into their beaks and feathers. Their wings were tucked into their chests, but their eyes glared at visitors.

I leaned closer to inspect them when the front door swung open.

A squat man bent at the waist, revealing the balding nature of his head. His mustache was the thickest I'd ever seen. It curled upward at the ends in the same way that I gave an extra loop to the letter y when I wrote. His head twitched just a tad in what I thought might be a bow, and he held the door open as we all entered the manor.

I found myself on an ornate rug with maroon swirls linked together to create intricate patterns. A large wooden table was set up across the entrance with an ornamental jardinière filled with green fronds extending from the center. The fern was so clearly alive in comparison to the garden by the fountain that I decided to take note of these too.

But before I could so much as turn my head to either side, Victor placed himself in front of me.

Up close, his eyes gleamed. His pupils darted left and right, examining my face as if I were a new cardboard insert for his zoetrope. He wanted to know how I spun, if I disrupted his collection of birds' wings spreading or toy soldiers marching.

"She has got some very bright eyes," he declared.

I took a step back, attempting to find relief in Mr. van Kirk's coattails. It was rather rude that he was addressing Mr. van Kirk as if I wasn't there, and I didn't like being stared at so closely.

"I thank you not to frighten her," he told Victor coolly.

Victor turned his head, abashed. "My apologies. Charlotte, is it?"

I meant to answer "yes," but I was distracted by Mr. van Kirk giving instructions to his butler. He was speaking of mail, clothing, rooms, and that evening's meal. I was exhausted from being woken early, and I could've done with a short rest and light refreshment, but I didn't think it was my place to request either.

Victor cleared his throat. His lips had formed a slightly crooked smile, and his head was inclined just so.

"Welcome home."

Soon after, Mr. van Kirk and Victor left me in the butler's care. The butler led me down the hall without a word. The walls were lined with elaborate hangings so tall that I had to stand on my toes in order to reach the tops of them. The portraits were equally intimidating, featuring what looked to be a long line of descendants of the van Kirks. Each background was darker than the last, from maroon to plum to black on black, so that their suits and gowns blended in with the brushstrokes.

None of their faces were welcoming or familiar. I paused every once in a while to return their stares and even attempted to fix a portrait that was atilt. But the butler fixed me with a steely look that warned me to keep moving, so I let my heels touch the ground and kept my head down too.

He led me up a winding staircase, past multiple closed doors, and around sharp corners, though we never stopped for long. Light shone beneath some doors, and I longed to explore them. I asked him every time, "What's behind that door?" But he made no reply.

Finally, I said, "May I ask what your name is?"

He came to a stop and faced me, straightening the lapels of his jacket. The creak of floorboards and rustling movement sounded from an open door nearby, but I couldn't see inside from where we stood. His voice was surprisingly gentle.

"Williams, miss."

I looked around and spotted a portrait of Mr. van Kirk above my head. He looked much the same except his hair was fuller and it gleamed in the dark. Next to his was a portrait of an astute strawberry-blond woman.

Williams cleared his throat, and I turned my attention back to him.

"That cannot be your Christian name," I said.

"No, miss."

I didn't understand why Williams was so secretive. I'd tell him my Christian name if he didn't already know it.

Williams's face softened. Even the edges of his mustache seemed to uncurl as his lips formed a small smile. He bent, just a little, so that his face was level with mine.

"You're a young lady now, Miss Charlotte. 'Williams' will do just fine."

Before I could ask anything else, he stepped into view of the open door. The room was covered in off-white silks and frills. The plain colors were offset by wooden bedposts and an ornate dresser. The window looked out toward the grounds with the sun's rays breaking through eggshell curtains.

"Your room, Miss Charlotte," he announced.

"Mine?" I repeated.

"Indeed," he said, bowing toward a shadow emerging from behind the door. "Lady van Kirk."

The woman looked very much like the woman in

the portrait next to Mr. van Kirk's in the hall. She was dressed in an apple-green gown with a sweetheart neckline. A copious amount of glass beads adorned it, so much so that I imagined the light reflecting against them blinding Williams if he turned the wrong way.

"Ah," Mrs. van Kirk murmured. "She has arrived. Wonderful."

Mrs. van Kirk's voice was nothing like her husband's. It was high-pitched, and she spoke quickly, so that her words jumbled together into one breath of air; it was sweet, too, almost sickly. Her eyes roamed over me.

I took a step into the room, clutching my skirts.

Williams coughed, rather indiscreetly.

I felt pink creeping up the side of my neck, and recalling my manners, I curtseyed.

Mrs. van Kirk smiled in turn, revealing her extra-white teeth. "Hello, Charlotte. It is a pleasure to meet you. I am Dorothea van Kirk, the lady of the manor. I was ensuring that the maids have made the room to our standards. It has not been in use in quite a while, you understand."

I didn't have a maid, nor did I have a room like this one, so I didn't understand. But I nodded.

"Do come in," she urged, beckoning me closer with a flick of her wrist. "You may get settled here, and someone will fetch you when it is time to eat. We dine relatively early, but I am sure you will grow used to it in time."

I thought this request odd, since I was already in the room, but I stepped more fully into it. "Thank you."

"You are most welcome," she replied stiffly, stepping toward the door. "I understand that you have begun your schooling in your…previous home."

I nodded.

"You arrived earlier than we anticipated, but we will send for a governess to monitor the rest of your schooling no later than the end of the week. Whomever we hire will accompany you throughout your day-to-day activities."

Before I could respond, she had swept out of the room with a short, "Good day." I could hear the swishing of her skirts down the length of the hall until she presumably reached the staircase. Williams informed me that he'd send someone to help me dress, and then he closed the door.

Until it was time to dine, I saw no one but a stout woman who helped me dress in silence. I asked her numerous questions about whether the gown was supposed to itch so much and if we couldn't fix my hair in a less tight manner. In an attempt to adjust my hair, I yanked a pin out, and she rebuked me.

Williams came to fetch me once I was ready, led me to the correct room, and then left me to stand near the head of the dining room table. The room itself was long and formal, capable of accommodating at least twenty guests comfortably. I began to count each chair that had been set out—*one, two, three, four*—but Mrs. van Kirk interrupted me.

"Will you be seated, Charlotte?" she said pointedly.

She sat on the left side of the head of the table, and she inclined her head toward the chair two seats in on the right side. The first chair, I assumed, was reserved for Victor, while the seat at the head was for no other than Mr. van Kirk himself.

As soon as I lowered myself onto the chair, Victor took the seat next to mine. The chair was hard and uncomfortable, forcing me to sit upright. I wiggled around in it, but I couldn't find a position to settle in.

I thought I saw Victor eyeing me warily, but I tried to ignore him. He hadn't grown used to sitting in chairs that sunk with your weight or material so faded that the design could've been anything at all.

His stare drew Mrs. van Kirk's attention, and she scrutinized me.

"Must you do that?" she asked.

Immediately, I stopped.

I glanced around the room for a reprieve, only to spot Mr. van Kirk entering the room. Williams held the door open for him, and Mr. van Kirk walked straight to his seat. He looked in good spirits as he surveyed the small party.

Mrs. van Kirk addressed me, her tone less harsh. "I hope you have found your room to your liking, Charlotte. Settled in now, are you?"

"Yes, I have," I responded. "Thank you. It's a beautiful room."

"A beautiful home," Mrs. van Kirk amended, straightening her fork so that the prongs aligned with the top of the other utensils.

Mr. van Kirk's gaze swung to his wife, but I couldn't read it. She didn't meet his eyes at first. But when he addressed her to ask her about her day, her head snapped up, and she spoke quickly. "My day was quite uneventful. I made sure that the room was ready for Charlotte's arrival and that the menu for dinner was adequate."

"And yours, Victor?"

Victor stared at the empty place in front of him. "Adequate."

"A man of few words," Mr. van Kirk murmured. "Shall we eat?"

The courses arrived then, one after another. First was savory soup, which was so hot upon arrival that I burned the tip of my tongue. Second was chicken fricassee served with rice, and the thought of licking my plate briefly crossed my mind. Third was a plate filled with vegetables that I ate, though I noticed Victor pushing his around his plate. Fourth was citrus ice, and fifth was dinner rolls with sweet cream butter. By the time we reached the sixth and last course, I was so full I thought I'd never be able to eat again. But the jams, jellies, and sweet pickles were too good to resist.

The conversation was stilted while we were eating.

Only Mr. van Kirk spoke without hesitation. He asked me if I found each course to my liking, and I responded every time that I thought the food was positively delightful. Mrs. van Kirk occasionally took my response as an opportunity to tell me about other dishes that were much more delightful from all over the world.

"I shall ask Molly to prepare a cake soon. The one with the fruit preserves, perhaps," she mused.

"That cake is my favorite," Victor said, his eyes wide.

Mrs. van Kirk's face lit up. "Is it, dear? We shall have it then."

Mr. van Kirk turned to me. "Is there anything you would like to have, Charlotte?"

"I would not know. I have not had the opportunity to try most of the food we have spoken of," I answered truthfully. "I think I would like mince pies immensely though. Or sweet rolls would do for the rest of my days."

Mr. van Kirk smiled at me encouragingly. "I am awfully fond of sweet rolls myself."

The conversation came to a lull not long after. I didn't mind it, since I was beginning to feel the exhaustion set in. The combination of moving into Ivywood Manor and enjoying a meal larger than I'd seen in my entire life was draining.

Mr. van Kirk was the first to rise from his chair, citing work as his reason for leaving. Mrs. van Kirk stood next and said she'd grown tired due to the excitement of the day's events. Victor rose almost instantly after Mrs. van

Kirk, but he gave no indication of where he was going. I was last to rise.

With my feet dragging, I trudged up the stairs. I miraculously found my room without a hitch and closed the door behind me. Then I plopped down on my bed, still in the clothes I dined in, and dreamed of ravens circling my head.

Part I

January 1885

THAT MORNING, THE SUN'S RAYS TOUCHED EVERY SPOTLESS CORNER OF MY ROOM. I COULD HEAR JANE, MY LADY'S MAID, BUSTLING around. Her feet shuffled across the floor, drawers opened and closed, and curtains slid across their rods. I turned over in hope of shading my eyes from the brightness.

"Miss Charlotte," Jane called.

I opened my eyes a fraction and recognized Jane's backside. "Is it terribly late, Jane?"

"Not terribly, no," she replied. "But you ought to get up about now."

I began to close my eyes again, but the urgency in Jane's voice gave me pause.

"Miss Charlotte," she repeated. "The young master is s'posed to arrive today, remember? He caught us all by surprise, arriving in the dead of night instead. And with a young lady, for goodness' sake."

At this reminder, I sat up.

Not long after arriving at Ivywood Manor, I'd resigned myself to the workings of the household. The texture of every square foot of the estate and the names of every portrait in the hall were etched in my brain, reminding me where I belonged. I learned early on that Victor would inherit the van Kirks' fortune, and he never let me forget that I was lucky to be taken in at all. Often, he pointed to my last name—Herring—to establish the obvious differences between us, though it was unnecessary.

I saw our differences without the mention of any names. Victor had been granted a seat at the men's table to play cards, while I'd sat on the couch pricking my finger in my pursuit of the art of needlework. When the men had grown bored of their game, I'd been urged to play the pianoforte for their entertainment. If I'd preferred to practice French, flower arranging, or reading, I'd been lectured about being a good host.

Although I'd willingly engaged in arguments with Victor on the subject of appropriate feminine behavior, the consequences hadn't always been pleasant. I'd watched as Victor trailed after the men when they went shooting, and he'd reported me to Mrs. van Kirk whenever I so much as looked at a hunting rifle for too long. She'd threatened to lock me in my room without supper, and the smirk on his face when he'd heard of my punishment had enraged me.

Even after I'd passed marrying age at eighteen, Victor continued to claim that he was the restless one.

He'd often make long trips into town when he wasn't obliged to study, preferring to be away from Ivywood Manor. When he was home, he'd kept to his room and emerged only to dine with the family. He'd been such poor company that Mr. van Kirk briefly considered sending him away to visit relatives and keep him occupied, but Mrs. van Kirk had protested vehemently against it.

Victor had detailed his intent to go abroad on a grand tour of Europe years ago. But rather than coming home with a fiancée, marrying, and inheriting the estate as was expected, he'd stayed away and wrote home sporadically.

I wondered whether he would look much the same upon his return. He was twenty-seven now, after all. Perhaps he'd found a new fashion of dress more to his liking or had picked up a bit of an accent. Mrs. van Kirk would very much dislike both.

Jane lightly tapped my arm. "Time to get dressed, miss."

She laid out my garments: a robin-blue walking dress next to starched stays and stockings. She stretched her hand out to have me stand, and I took it. As she helped me dress, she murmured for me to lift my arm or straighten my back.

While she did so, I pictured Victor—the paleness of him, as if I spent twice the amount of time in the sun as he did. The frame of his body was much like Mr. van Kirk's but thinner and lankier. He walked with exaggerated strides and angular, swinging arms that hinted at a discomfort with the length of his limbs.

"Miss?" Jane said, prompting me to step into my stockings.

I inquired, "Does Victor look much changed?"

"I have yet to see him. Shall we braid your hair before we fret about the young master?"

"Do you think he'll be wed?" I wondered. "I would not mind it truthfully if he did. He mentioned a woman in one of his letters, did he not? Lucille was her name."

Jane paid no mind to my questions about Victor or his potential bride. She was too busy twisting and turning the strands of my hair into an artfully created bird's nest. I watched her in the mirror, imagining lovebirds making their home on my head, pecking at beads like birdseed carefully glued in straight lines on pins.

"You're all set," she declared.

I thanked Jane and started down the stairs. The smell of freshly baked bread floated in the air. I thought of seeds again and wondered whether lovebirds were anything like ravens. Would either species feed on the crumbs if I left a small pile outside of my window?

My thoughts were quickly interrupted by the appearance of Victor and a woman.

He was so clearly unchanged that I wondered why I'd ever thought he'd be otherwise. His coloring was as pale as ever, and though his body looked to have become almost lankier, his features were the same. To my surprise, he stared at me as if I were a stranger for a few prolonged seconds.

Then he came forward and pressed my hands between his. "Charlotte."

"Victor, your travels have treated you well, I trust," I said evenly. "We are all so glad that you have returned."

"As am I," he replied, stepping aside. "I would like to introduce you to Miss Lucille King. Father might have mentioned the King name. Her father is in Parliament."

Lucille was a petite blonde with blue eyes reminiscent of a porcelain doll's. She had a small nose and lips just thick enough to be satisfactory and not overly plump. She was draped in layers of frill so thick that the garment bulged outward, which she couldn't possibly sit in comfortably.

I dipped into a curtsy.

"It's a pleasure to meet you," Lucille said, repeating the gesture. "Victor has told me so much about you."

"The pleasure is mine," I replied. "Will you be staying long?"

Victor offered his arm to Lucille, intent upon leading her to the dining room. "Yes, I think I must stay awhile. Lucille, as well. I would like to give her the grand tour of Ivywood Manor."

I followed. "Was it a prosperous journey? Did you gain much from it? I am certain you must have."

Victor waved his hand in dismissal. "We must discuss

it later. It's hardly anything for ladies' ears. I'd much rather hear about the goings-on here. Has there been much excitement while I was away?"

I bristled at his unwillingness to share, momentarily pausing in my steps. "Anticipating your homecoming, certainly."

"Certainly," he repeated.

Lucille's eyes focused on Victor, then me. "I am certain Victor will regale you with all his stories soon."

"Of course," I agreed.

We arrived at the dining room, where freshly cooked pastries sprinkled with herbs awaited us. Mr. and Mrs. van Kirk occupied their usual seats at the table. Mr. van Kirk held the newspaper in his hands, while Mrs. van Kirk chattered at him. Upon spotting Victor, Mrs. van Kirk stopped speaking immediately. She rose to embrace him, murmuring his name; all the while, Lucille was forced to stand politely to the side.

"Welcome home, Victor," Mr. van Kirk said by way of greeting. "Will you take a seat, Miss King?"

Mrs. van Kirk released Victor at the sound of Lucille's name and ushered her toward the seat next to mine. Victor took his seat straight across from Lucille, and Lucille thanked both Mr. and Mrs. van Kirk for their hospitality.

"Your journey was not too taxing, I hope. We were not expecting you so late at night." The tone of Mr. van Kirk's voice was scolding.

"Not at all, Father," Victor responded quickly. "We simply could not keep away any longer."

"I am sure," he said. "Your mother has been quite worried about you. You have ordered a great many things to be placed in this household. The prices appear to exceed your usual allowances."

It was not the first occasion on which Mr. van Kirk had brought up Victor's spending. A few days prior to Victor's arrival, Mrs. van Kirk had inquired what Mr. van Kirk's plans were for the day. He told her that Jones, his solicitor, had been in touch about the numerous furniture pieces and trinkets that Victor had ordered. Her response had been to sulk, stirring her cup of coffee furiously until drops spilled onto the tablecloth.

The stain was still there, and Mrs. van Kirk rubbed the spot with her napkin twice as if believing it would disappear with a little force. "Oh! We should not speak of money at the table."

Victor's lips pressed together into a tight line. "Everything is in order, Father."

Mr. van Kirk scoffed.

I nearly asked what Victor meant by that when Mr. van Kirk caught my eye. He shook his head infinitesimally, and I closed my mouth again. He didn't speak much after that, except to comment on the delightful nature of the breakfast spread Molly had prepared.

Mrs. van Kirk, on the other hand, pressed Victor about his travels. He replied in short, cross sentences that his travels had been perfectly satisfactory. Disappointed with his responses, Mrs. van Kirk moved on to politely inquiring after Lucille's family and her own travels in Europe.

Lucille's face took on a look of surprise whenever she was addressed. Her attention was focused on the sound of her fork scraping against the plate or daintily dabbing at the corners of her lips with a napkin. She answered Mrs. van Kirk's questions eloquently but refused to elaborate.

The entire meal dragged on with the sound of utensils hitting the table, glasses being raised to lips, and Mrs. van Kirk's interrogation. I stole furtive glances at Victor, who glared at Mr. van Kirk, though Mr. van Kirk paid Victor no attention. I was quite certain that he was upset at the lack of warm welcome he'd received from Mr. van Kirk, and he was as spoiled as ever to expect it. If it were not for Mrs. van Kirk's chatter, breakfast would have been a decidedly silent affair.

LATER THAT AFTERNOON, MRS. VAN KIRK, LUCILLE, and I were gathered in the informal drawing room. Lucille was seated on the settee across from Mrs. van Kirk and shrank away whenever Mrs. van Kirk reached over to grasp her hands. I thought Mrs. van Kirk was celebrating Victor's wedded bliss rather prematurely, so I kept to myself near the window on the other side of the room.

"Lucille, Victor tells us that you have a talent for playing the pianoforte," Mrs. van Kirk cooed.

Her latest pronouncement made Lucille blush. I noticed that she blushed with a startling frequency, as if it took great courage for her to acknowledge any words said to her. Was she eighteen or nineteen? She looked young.

Lucille was now patiently combatting Mrs. van Kirk's requests for her to play the pianoforte, and I admired her resilience. I most certainly would have been worn down by now. Not that Mrs. van Kirk thought very highly of my piano-playing abilities.

"Oh! Why do you not sing?" Mrs. van Kirk suggested.

"I am certain that my voice is not all that great. There are plenty of other young ladies who possess a much more refined voice than mine," Lucille said. "Perhaps Charlotte could play for us."

Mrs. van Kirk looked so utterly offended at the suggestion that I had to restrain myself from laughing.

"I am afraid that I am much out of practice," I said, "and there are many who play better than I."

"I shall go without for today then," Mrs. van Kirk sighed.

A look of utter relief spread across Lucille's face. Her eyes softened, and the lines around her lips disappeared entirely. She began to peruse the drawing room.

But Mrs. van Kirk was not satisfied. "If there is to be no entertainment, what am I to do? Shall I rest?"

"Are you unwell?" I inquired, halfhearted. "The time you rest is entirely up to you, I assure you."

Mrs. van Kirk scowled, turning resolutely toward the other end of the room. She concentrated particularly hard on penning a letter to one of her dearest friends, to whom, she said, she was indebted for all the entertainment the other lady's daughters provided. But she never did leave.

Lucille wandered toward me, glancing out the window. "It's a beautiful day."

"Yet we are inside. Why is that?" I returned. "Do you play so well, Miss King?"

Lucille shook her head. "I am not as accomplished as Victor has made me out to be, I am afraid. I practice, but I am not exceptionally skilled in any occupation, and I get dreadfully nervous playing in front of others."

"I do believe you are being modest," I countered.

"I am not," Lucille swore. "And please, do call me Lucille."

I beamed. "Lucille, I do believe you are being modest then."

Lucille laughed daintily. The sound evoked images of fairies and trails of magic dust. She appeared so lighthearted and honest that I pictured her flitting around the room.

"I hope you do not find this too forward of me to ask. But are you and Victor getting along well?" I asked.

Lucille's laugh faded a bit. "Yes, we are. We were introduced through my father while Victor was traveling. My father was so taken with Victor that he asked him to extend his stay. He allowed Victor to escort me to several outings."

"Taken…as were you?" I wondered.

Lucille picked at a bead that was coming off her dress before lifting her lips and answering. "Yes, as was I."

I wasn't sure that she meant it.

"I've grown up very sheltered, you see," Lucille explained quickly. "Father's approval means the world to me. There aren't many suitors he allows me to be near. He introduced me to many a different kind of man from Parliament."

"They are very sophisticated men—those in Parliament," I guessed. "Well, so I have heard. I do not often venture far from Ivywood."

"It is not all that exciting," she sighed. This time, her eyebrows mashed together as the loose bead fell off her dress and into her hands. "Father chose him."

"You mean, you would not have chosen Victor?" I asked, incredulous.

She shook her head. "No, but Victor has been quite charming. He doted on my father to a great degree in order to meet me. I am sure we will be very happy in time."

I did my best not to gape. "How can you be sure?"

"I cannot," she answered truthfully. "But I can be optimistic. Father says it is a good match, and I trust him implicitly."

A pause.

"I should get this fixed," she said, holding up the bead for inspection. "Do you not agree?"

AFTER MANY COMPLAINTS ISSUED BY MRS. VAN KIRK, Victor agreed to join us in the drawing room and relate his travels in the afternoon. He chose to sit on the settee, placing some distance between himself and Lucille. I couldn't help but notice that she shifted away from him, though Victor didn't seem bothered.

"Do tell us," Mrs. van Kirk urged.

Victor made a show of considering her request, shaking his head and feigning modesty. It didn't take more than a few more sentences from Mrs. van Kirk to change his mind. He waited a little longer, though, until Lucille urged him to speak as well.

"Please do," I added. "We are all looking forward to it so."

He shot me an irritated look. "I shall…"

Victor spent hours recounting his time in Paris, speaking of a pleasurable stay in Italy, and detailing a more cautious residence in Rome. He praised a highly skilled man who'd taught him to fence, named a great many paintings, and expanded upon tours of elaborate sculpture gardens. These activities were for the wealthiest circles of society in which he'd found himself, and he clearly loathed leaving it.

"The sophistication of Europe's high society is

unparalleled," he claimed. "Hardly a match for society in town. I assure you I will be visiting often."

"I am sure!" Mrs. van Kirk readily agreed. "But is it so that you will leave so soon?"

"I will remain for a while, but would you not agree with me, Lucille?" he pressed.

She wrung her hands awkwardly at being directly addressed. "Yes."

Satisfied, he continued with his story. Mrs. van Kirk interrupted him with strong exclamations at his descriptions, claiming that she could picture the scenes perfectly. Whenever I questioned her enthusiasm, she reminded me that I'd never been to Europe, so I couldn't understand the memories Victor was evoking.

"I would think so," Victor declared. "That is what I meant to do, after all."

In order to demonstrate the high socialites Victor had walked among, he then brought out many of the gifts he'd brought home. There were snuffboxes and paperweights from all the places he'd visited. He said the statues he'd ordered were yet to arrive, but he was certain they'd come any day.

I pretended to admire the items along with Lucille and Mrs. van Kirk, but there was not much to remark upon. I was certain that these purchases were responsible for his exceeding his allowance. Though the van Kirks did well and Victor had always enjoyed possessing that which was in fashion, I had never seen him throw away money to this careless extent in the past.

Victor ended his tale by informing us that the last project he'd undertaken was a commissioned painting. It featured himself in Europe to display his well-traveled glory. I knew that, if anywhere, it would have to go in his own quarters.

On the following day, I woke to the sun rising above the horizon. The clouds were slow to part from one another. I thought to draw the curtains shut, but I remembered the basket of English ivy hanging near the windowsill and left it open. I spent a few minutes watching the sky change before I snuck down into the kitchen to nip a bite to eat.

The kitchen was a dull-looking room with stone walls making up its circumference. Large bronze pots twice as old as the cooks who used them sat on the stovetop, and containers filled with flour, sugar, salt, and pepper lined the shelves. Despite the kitchen's appearance, I always felt that it was one of the more magical rooms in the manor because I never felt a need to put on airs. The cooks let me flit in and out, never bothering to scold me for the state of my clothes or hair, unlike when I was in the family's presence.

Molly, a permanent fixture in the kitchen and one of my favorite people in the household, was already awake. Her apron was dusted with flour from freshly made dough, and her face was scrunched up in concentration as she searched for something on the shelves. She was standing on her tiptoes with her head craned at an odd angle.

I knocked on the wall, and Molly whirled around.

"Oh, lord. You gave me a scare," she scolded, placing a firm hand on her hip. "You're up at the crack of dawn, aren't you?"

"What are you looking for?" I asked.

"Thyme," she muttered. "Never seem to have enough of it."

"I can grow herbs for you, Molly."

"That's not your job, is it?" she said, shifting jars from one side of the shelf to the other. "Though it'd be mighty helpful."

I went to Molly's side and retrieved the thyme for her, contemplating the best location in the manor for herbs to grow. I'd acquired a Wardian case of relative size that I'd been using to experiment with growing flowers indoors. The case was in the guest room next to my own because Mrs. van Kirk despised seeing me tend to it. But I could already imagine putting it to use for Molly's store of ingredients.

"I'll need to purchase seeds, but after, I can start growing them right away."

Molly gave her thanks and then continued to go about her business. I watched her massage the thyme into a ball of dough and fold the mixture in on itself. Occasionally, she glanced up to check what I was doing as if I were still nine and couldn't be trusted near the ingredients.

"What are you after today, Miss Charlotte?" Molly asked finally. "Tea? Biscuits to start off the morning?"

"You wouldn't mind if I fixed myself a plate, would you, Molly?"

"Don't matter if I mind, does it?" she replied, handing me a clean plate. "You would swipe food anyhow. You would think you're going hungry."

I laughed. "I am not."

"You're lucky Mr. van Kirk keeps his breakfast hours early, else you wouldn't have anything to eat," Molly reminded me with a wave of her wooden spoon. "How's the girl?"

"What girl?"

"Come now, Miss Charlotte. We all know the young master brought home a young lady. Had to send up some warm milk for her to get to sleep last night."

I began filling my plate. "Victor has not spoken of marriage yet. But I do believe he means to marry her, Molly."

Molly filled a cup with tea and handed it to me. "He's at that age, I suppose. Marriage, head of the estate… You could have done the same."

I nearly dropped the cup. "There are no advantages to the institution of marriage for me."

"Are there not?" she countered.

"No," I said, shaking my head. "I shall be a spinster without inheritance."

She pursed her lips. "Do you like her much?"

"She seems a pleasant sort. I do not know that Victor is thinking much about that."

"If it is convenient, dear, I doubt it matters. It's especially convenient with the type of background she has got, if the rumors are right."

I swirled my tea. "Is that why it sounds as if he courted her father as much as her? How utterly depressing a thought that is, Molly."

"Yes, well," Molly said, shaking her head. "Ah, this conversation is putting me in a right state. Go on upstairs and eat your food. Keep us informed about Victor, will you? I need to know ahead of time if I am to prepare a wedding feast."

Not long after breakfast, I determined to ride around the estate. I always obtained more current information about Ivywood Manor from the tenants than Mr. van Kirk. I enjoyed visiting them in the cottages, foregoing the cover of a parasol and playing with the children.

It was my habit to spend time outdoors, even as a child. If I was not riding, I inhaled whiffs of dirt and observed the sad state of the gardens, especially in the winter months. If the day was not suited for either of those activities, I watched Molly craft dishes in the kitchen and begged her to teach me how to do the same.

Mrs. van Kirk took increasing issue with my time outdoors as I grew older. She made snide comments about my skin becoming darker, comparing an ivory tablecloth to my olive hand. Or she spoke of her strenuous efforts to avoid the harsh rays of the sun, as if it were a practice that I'd forgotten how to perform.

I couldn't bring myself to say anything in response.

To appease her, I occasionally worked to hone the few skills I had with the written word. I thumbed through philosophy books and ledgers alike, making notations and recording my observations on particularly interesting passages. I even took my interest in gardening indoors, where neither the weather nor Mrs. van Kirk affected the pastime. I might not have been destined to inherit the estate, but that didn't mean I had no interest in the affairs of the van Kirks.

I dressed in my riding habit that day: a simple gathering of navy-blue material. Upon seeing me, Lucille inquired whether she could trouble me so much as to accompany me. I could hardly deny her request, and once it was agreed upon, Victor insisted on joining us. I was certain that he'd prefer to go hunting, but I didn't voice any protest.

I waited for Lucille and Victor by the stables. The groomsman, Charles, had readied my mare, a red roan horse named Willow that Mr. van Kirk had gifted me. She was a solid-hoofed, strong beast with a flowing mane and tail, and when I rode her, I felt as if I rode flames—red-hot embers licking blades of grass until they turned to dirt.

Charles had brought out another two horses and

readied them by the time Lucille and Victor strolled to the stables. Lucille wore a riding habit of a similar fashion to my own, while Victor's riding apparel appeared to be another recent purchase. Lucille's fingers shook as she ran them lightly over the other mare's neck. Victor looked unhappy grabbing hold of his steed's reins.

"You need not accompany us if you do not wish to, Victor," Lucille said gently.

"No, no," he replied, brusque. "I do not mind it."

I thought Victor did indeed mind it, as he'd never found enjoyment in touring the estate.

Ivywood Manor's land consisted of a home farm, cottages, stables, and more trees and lawn than I imagined anyone knew what to do with. The home farm kept the manor mostly self-sufficient when the weather permitted. The tenants occupied the cottages around the estate and farmed their surrounding land, while the stables were cared for by the servants. The trees continued to grow, and their branches continued to extend, no matter the circumstance. The lawn remained empty but for blades of grass.

Victor used to inquire, "Why are you showing me this, Father?"

Mr. van Kirk would purse his lips. "When I am no longer here, you will inherit the estate, and you must know it well. If you do not, you might run it to the ground. And it is good for Charlotte to understand, too."

Victor's eyes would dart toward me and narrow a fraction.

I'd ignore him and concentrate on the sound of horses neighing from afar. I'd known that if someone were to run it to the ground, it would be Victor with his disregard for estate matters. He found them tedious.

Thinking it might be best to take a turn or two around the grounds, I mounted Willow and faced east. But once the other two mounted their horses, Victor motioned for us to follow him in the opposite direction.

I was most perturbed at this sudden change.

Victor, however, sat stiff on his horse and led us at an exceedingly slow trot around the estate. He paused to point out rocks or dips in the ground to be avoided after he'd nearly stumbled in them. I, of course, knew the land more intimately, and if I didn't know better, I would've sworn I saw Lucille directing her mare to follow mine.

"This," Victor announced, "is one of the cottages."

The cottage's timber walls were worn down by the wind and rain, resembling the color of a dirt-flecked yellow dress. But the diamond windowpanes were kept relatively clean, revealing the homely atmosphere within. The tenants kept them lively with frequently cut foliage.

Jack, the groundskeeper, was pulling dead leaves from the bushes. His fingers were stained brown by the dirt, but he handled the discarded leaves as if they were crystallized glass. I called out to ask him if he needed any help, but he staunchly refused.

"The groundskeeper," Victor informed Lucille.

"He lives with his wife," I added. "They have no children, but they care for most everyone else's."

"Jack," Lucille repeated, turning her attention toward me. "His wife is…?"

"Helen," I answered.

Though I'd done nothing to provoke her anger, Helen had disliked me from the first. She often made snide comments when Jack spoke to me. She, like a few of the other servants, felt that I didn't deserve the same respect they gave Victor.

I'd asked Mr. van Kirk on more than one occasion what I could do to gain her trust, but he'd told me not to bother. He said that not everyone could see past my adoption. Not many families took in children, as it often caused quite the scandal, and some servants lived for their master's reputation.

Oftentimes, I wondered whether my last name made a difference. I'd asked Mr. van Kirk once why he'd chosen to let me keep Herring as opposed to assuming van Kirk. He'd reminded me that I had nothing from my birth family, and he'd decided against taking away the one thing my mother had given me.

There was no denying that he was right about the issue of my adoption. I tried to be kind to Helen whenever I happened upon her. I even sent down homemade biscuits after much prodding at Molly to give me leave of her oven. But no matter what, Helen refused to say more than two curt words to me, and I couldn't imagine my name changing her behavior toward me.

To speak with Jack, I excused myself and dismounted. I urged him to let me pick up some of the dead twigs. He refused once more, saying I would dirty my hands. But eventually he stepped aside and let me collect a bundle to be discarded.

As I handed him the twigs, I could hear the scuffing of hooves against the ground. I looked up to find Victor had led his horse toward us. He was staring in the direction of Jack's cottage with his hands holding the reins tight.

I turned to find Helen's head framed within the cottage's window. Her face was pinched and her eyes small. When I met her gaze, she pivoted away from the window and disappeared behind a wall.

I thanked Jack for caring for the lawn so well, and Victor wrinkled his nose in disgust.

"You should not concern yourself with those sorts of things," he muttered. "It's hardly ladylike, and Lucille should not be subjected to your antics."

Jack seemed sufficiently chastised, as he immediately averted his gaze from both of us.

I brushed off my hands before remounting Willow. "You could have continued on. Besides, you should not concern yourself with the sort of things I am doing if it upsets you so."

Rather than respond, Victor whipped his head around. He urged his horse on to the next stop, and Lucille timidly went with him. I followed at a much slower pace, only partly listening to Victor pointing out unique aspects of his surroundings that he was hardly familiar with himself.

Lucille nodded politely or asked questions when it was required of her. Sometimes, she turned to ask me questions about the people who lived at Ivywood Manor. I answered her, but otherwise I kept quiet.

"Do you ride often, Charlotte?" Lucille asked.

I shook my head. "Not very. Only to pass the time on pleasant days or to visit some of the tenants."

A tiny crinkle formed between Lucille's eyebrows. "Is that so?"

"Yes," I replied. "Does it seem that I do? I ride well with Willow, if that is what you are referring to. She has been with me for quite some time now."

"Ah, no," she said, her face flushing pink. "I thought that perhaps you rode often. Your skin is so very tan, and I thought it might be attributed to the pleasantness of the outdoors. I do not wander outdoors all that often."

At the sound of her words, Victor interrupted. "Speaking of tans, shall we go back now? I have some things to attend to. I prefer my skin stay on the lighter side. You should as well, Lucille."

I bristled at the insult. My skin was certainly of no concern to him, and to imply otherwise was crass on his part. I tried to remember all the good manners my governess had attempted to instill in me, but I shied away from accommodating Victor; he'd been away for so long, and I'd been so very content without him.

February 1885

As it was a journey of great length, the van Kirks did not travel into town often. On one of those occasions, I'd accompanied them to fetch some scarves for Mrs. van Kirk, and the shopkeeper had called me a nasty name. I hadn't heard it, but I'd seen Mrs. van Kirk mouthing the words "half" and something indiscernible under her breath.

I hadn't been able to make any sense of it at the time, but Mrs. van Kirk had made it abundantly clear that she'd prefer it if I didn't go into town. I hadn't minded so much, though I had missed the change in scenery during the summer months when being outdoors looked so appealing. Victor hadn't been allowed to go into town often either because he was engaged with his studies, which had made me feel infinitely better about the situation.

I'd watched him throw a vase at the front door in

protest once. It flew from his fingertips and hit the ground with a deafening crash. The pieces of the vase and fronds from within it had spilled onto the ground. Then, the small puddle of water had begun to seep into the floor as Victor flattened the fern beneath the sole of his foot.

Mr. and Mrs. van Kirk had exchanged words about Victor's behavior. Mr. van Kirk had attributed it to a lack of discipline, while Mrs. van Kirk had said he was only prone to boyish tendencies. Mr. van Kirk had reminded her that he'd never done the same.

The journey of going into town gave me no joy like it used to, but Mrs. van Kirk's disgust with town gossip was outweighed by her pride. She was so insistent on everyone attending Victor and Lucille that I was obliged to go, and I suspected it was because she wanted to visit the dressmaker's in search of wedding garments, though no wedding had yet been discussed. She refrained, however, from speaking of the matter on the way there.

Upon our arrival, Mr. van Kirk said that he had some business to attend to. Victor turned to head in another direction, but he was stopped by a reminder to settle some accounts. He unhappily followed his father to the solicitor's office and promised to be back in a jiffy to spend his money elsewhere.

Mrs. van Kirk led Lucille and I through town. She lingered in the hat shop, examining brims and feathers by pressing them a little too hard between her bony fingers. She peeked into one store for boots and shoes, though she didn't venture to try any on. Not until Lucille suggested that we enter a dressmaker's shop did Mrs. van Kirk's face light up.

Though the shop was not one that Mrs. van Kirk typically patronized, she was too excited by Lucille's suggestion to raise any objections. The dressmaker immediately greeted us at the door and fawned over all of us, speaking of Mrs. van Kirk's timeless beauty and Lucille's youth. She even complimented my ability to wear more colors than her other patrons, calling me an olive beauty.

Mrs. van Kirk and Lucille watched as she held gowns up to me, colored tea rose and fern green with beads and ruffles galore. I kept my attention riveted to the dressmaker, feeling abashed by how vocal she was. Other patrons began to stare, and I knew Mrs. van Kirk's temper was rising.

In order to appease Mrs. van Kirk, the dressmaker was forced to double her attentions back to her. Mrs. van Kirk still vowed that she wouldn't return to the shop when we exited the door. Lucille apologized profusely for choosing that shop, but Mrs. van Kirk waved her words away. She said that we would simply have to see our usual dressmaker instead, because Mrs. Simpson never displayed such poor manners.

We found Victor and Mr. van Kirk already seated in the carriage upon our return. They were both sulking, but their hunched shoulders couldn't surpass Mrs. van

Kirk's sullen attitude. Her face turned pale and her knuckles white when they asked how our shopping had gone. Mr. van Kirk asked her several times if she was well, and each time, Mrs. van Kirk replied that she was only thinking about some gowns that had not suited her.

When we returned, Mr. van Kirk pulled me aside and asked me how I was faring after the day's adventure. He said Mrs. van Kirk had informed him, after much insistence on his part, that the dressmaker had called me an olive beauty, and she was not mistaken. I'd grown up to be a charming young lady, and if anyone said otherwise, I should tell him straightaway.

I thought of olives, how I'd tasted the sourness and saltiness of the fruit on more than one occasion since arriving at the manor. I pictured them—dark purple, muddy green, black and smooth. I didn't understand how I fit the description.

But there was such genuine concern in his voice that I crossed my hand over my heart and promised that I would.

UNLIKE MOST PEOPLE, WHO ROSE AT THE FASHIONABLE hour, I preferred to start my days as soon as the light shone through my bedroom window. I readied myself for breakfast, sometimes popping my head into the kitchen to visit Molly. She shooed me away with a stern finger, and I sat at the dining room table buttering sweet rolls and sipping hot chocolate until someone else came down.

Like myself, Mr. van Kirk was an early riser. He settled his stomach with bacon and eggs while flipping through the morning paper. He paused between bites to comment on news from Parliament or ask what plans I had made for the day. But for the most part, we ate in companionable silence.

I'd learned quickly that Mrs. van Kirk didn't come down to breakfast until much later, and I could avoid being reprimanded simply by not being present. She made no qualms about the fact that we rarely crossed paths in the morning. Victor was quite the same.

By the time Mrs. van Kirk, Victor, and Lucille came down, I was strolling around the estate, and Mr. van Kirk was heading to his office to start the day. It was only Lucille who reminded us how unusual it was that she'd only seen me in the morning once or twice on days that I'd decided to sleep in a little. Even then, she commented, I didn't stay for long.

"I like to get an early start," I admitted.

"Is that so?" she asked, tilting her head. "I do prefer to be up a little earlier. What do you normally do after?"

"I usually take a short walk," I replied.

She mulled this information over. "Perhaps I'll join you one day."

And she did.

Only two days after our brief exchange about breakfast hours, Lucille joined Mr. van Kirk and I in the morning as if it were any other day. We both looked up from our plates in surprise, and she apologized for intruding. I promised her that it was no intrusion, and she felt the need to explain that she much preferred this hour to any other.

"It is always nice to have extra company," Mr. van Kirk assured her.

"Thank you," she murmured. "I hope you do not mind, Charlotte."

"Not at all!" I said truthfully. "I only did not expect it. I thought you'd prefer to eat with Victor and Mrs. van Kirk."

Her eyes darted away. "I…would, only, if I must admit, I do find your presence very settling to the nerves."

"Settling?" I echoed.

Mr. van Kirk smiled behind his paper. "Charlotte does have that effect on most people."

"Not all," I reminded him, recalling a few of the servants' faces as I passed them on the way to the kitchen that morning.

Mr. van Kirk gave me a curious glance. "Most."

Lucille heartily agreed that I was a pleasure to be around. She asked me numerous questions about Ivywood Manor and its inhabitants while she spread jam over her toast and swirled her tea. Mr. van Kirk deferred to me to answer her questions, and every time I paused to speak, I saw she waited to take her next bite. It was almost as if she were timing the pace of her meal with my own.

"I was hoping," she began, pressing the napkin lightly to her mouth, "that I might accompany you on your morning walk."

While I'd grown used to the solitary nature of my walks, I couldn't deny her. She seemed very hesitant to request it of me, and I could see no motive for her wishing to join me other than to get some air. I didn't mind her company either, so I assented.

I assumed that she might need to change or gather her things, but she was prepared for my answer. She was ready at the door with me as soon as we'd finished eating. There was a parasol already leaning against the coat closet to shade her head, too.

"Do you find me too forward?" she blurted as soon as we set out.

I paused. "Whatever do you mean?"

Her words came out in a quick jumble as she waved absentmindedly at her surroundings. "Inviting myself to an earlier breakfast and joining your morning walk."

"No, of course not."

She let out a sigh of relief. "I am glad."

"I must admit," I confessed, "that I find it a tad curious. I am not such delightful company, you know."

"Oh! I must disagree. It is very odd being in a new place alone, and you have been so kind to me. You never insist upon anything."

I thought she must have been referring to Mrs. van Kirk's attentions, but I knew better than to ask.

"Well, you are more than welcome to ask anything of me during your stay."

Suddenly, she grasped both my hands. "Thank you, Charlotte. You do not know how much that means to me."

I pressed her hands in return, speechless.

We said little of anything else after that. I showed her the area in front of the manor where I'd planted bulbs the previous autumn, and I pointed to the best spot to see the stars in the sky at night. She seemed to absorb every little detail of the countryside, not very used to being surrounded by nature, and I was more than happy to share it with her.

NOT LONG AFTER MY WALK WITH LUCILLE, I VERY rarely found myself alone. She continued to join Mr. van Kirk and me at breakfast. I took my walks with Lucille too, though she usually only went halfway to admire the beauty of the land before rejoining Victor and Mrs. van Kirk. Though they desired her presence, I soon found myself missing having someone to converse with.

Unfortunately, Victor noticed her fondness for me and began asking that I accompany him and Lucille on almost every occasion. Whether it was a long walk or a trip into town, my presence was requested. I'd been around the manor on horseback with them twice and watched them paint landscapes on four separate occasions. While I knew Lucille found my company comforting, any servant could have served the same purpose.

One day, I was on my way to the library when Victor intercepted me in the hallway. He was dressed in a hunter green suit, and his cuff links were missing, as if he'd darted away from his valet mid-dressing. His face gave me pause too, as he looked so anxious that I half believed an apparition would appear from a wall and place a ravaged hand on his shoulder.

"I have been searching for you all morning," he said.

Seeing as I'd left the breakfast table a mere hour ago, I said nothing.

"Yes, well," he continued, as if I'd spoken. "I have a favor to ask of you. Would you like to accompany Lucille and me for a walk?"

"A walk?" I repeated.

"A short walk."

"It's quite a gloomy day, is it not?" I pointed out, as even I had planned to stay indoors.

"Never you mind," he said, a little more forcefully. "You begin to sound like Lucille. I cannot court her if we are not to do any activities together."

"Certainly," I replied. "But I do not see why you must do those activities with me if you are courting her."

His face twisted into a grotesque sneer. "She is

more…open in your presence than she is without. Will you accompany us or not?"

I turned my head in search of anyone to rescue me from the conversation but found none. "Perhaps another day."

Victor made a sharp hissing sound. "You do not wish for me to be married?"

"I did not say that!" I protested. "What are you on about?"

He regained his composure, smoothed his hands over his suit, and murmured, "Nothing, nothing at all."

"I was looking forward to some quiet, that is all," I said slowly.

"Quiet," he repeated blandly. "Yes, certainly. Quiet. I am sure we will be perfectly content without you then."

He jumped.

Lucille had emerged from around the staircase and touched Victor on the shoulder. She'd jerked her hand back in surprise, and now she was cradling it to her chest. She was clothed in a robin-blue day gown, which was significantly less covered in jewels than her other garments.

"I apologize," she murmured. "I did not intend to startle you so."

But Victor had already resumed smoothing his suit. "No trouble at all. I was only inquiring whether Charlotte wished to join us."

Lucille titled her head and stared at me inquisitively. "Do you wish to accompany us?"

"She does not," Victor interrupted. "She is feeling out of sorts."

"Is that so?" Lucille asked. "Do you need me to fetch a doctor? We need not go on a walk at all. Or we could keep you company, could we not, Victor?"

Victor placed Lucille's arm over his own and shook his head. "No, that is quite unnecessary."

I nodded. "I only wanted some rest."

"You shan't do anything overly taxing?" Lucille asked, worry creasing her eyebrows. "We must go for a walk another day."

"Yes, another day," I conceded. "We will have many opportunities to do so, I am sure."

Victor tugged at Lucille's arm. "I daresay we will. Shall we go now then? We do not wish to interrupt Charlotte's day."

Lucille agreed that she didn't wish to be a bother. But I knew that Victor's comment was not nearly as concerned with my health as he claimed it to be. He was clearly agitated by my refusal to aid him in courting Lucille, and I wondered why it was so important that he marry Lucille—and soon.

By the time Victor and Lucille returned from their walk, I'd read a new French book, watered all the ferns in the manor, and readjusted the pebbles in the trays beneath the pot of begonias in the library. I lingered in the library, sitting on the edge of the chair across from Mr. van Kirk with the ornate ceramic pot between us.

In autumn, the pot had been filled with red, fibrous begonias before it had suffered from the change in season and winter's air. I'd asked Williams to discard the dying leaves and filled the pot with healthy cuttings. Now, I laid out two new seed packets in preparation for spring: one rhizomatous and the other tuberous begonias. I planned on growing white and pink blossoms as soon as the weather allowed, and I wanted to envision where I would place the new flowers.

"They'll grow to be quite pretty I think," I commented.

Mr. van Kirk glanced up from his papers and smiled. "I do agree. You possess skill when it comes to growing flowers, especially indoors."

I wrinkled my nose doubtfully. "I do not think I would go so far as to say that. Winter is the most difficult, and books only aid me to a certain point."

"What has brought you here today? I fear you've exhausted most of my gardening collection, Charlotte."

"Have I?" I asked, smiling. "I do believe you should purchase more books then. It would make me ever so happy."

Many joyful moments occurred when I spent time in the library with Mr. van Kirk. I was used to the scratch of fountain pen against paper and the rustling of Mr. van Kirk's arm moving across the desk. He grew used to my presence as well, sitting in the chair across from his or on the settee in the middle of the room, thumbing through books.

He dipped his head. "I will consider it, but only if you continue to grow flowers for the library."

"They bring you that much joy?"

"There were never many flowers inside the manor except for the rooms in which we had guests," he said thoughtfully.

I moved the ceramic pot on the desk, away from the direct sunlight. "Does Mrs. van Kirk dislike them so?"

"She enjoys ferns enough. Victor does not." He paused. "Speaking of Victor, did you not go out with him and Lucille today?"

"I did not," I informed him, turning the seed packets over in my hands. "He seems to be under the impression that by not accompanying them, I am hindering his chances at marriage. Does that not seem unusual to you?"

Mr. van Kirk pressed his lips together into a tight, disapproving line. "It's not unusual for Victor. He has gotten himself into quite some trouble."

"Financial trouble—?" I began to ask when two quick raps on the door stopped me.

"Come in," Mr. van Kirk called.

Williams opened the door to reveal Lucille in the very same robin blue day gown. Her eyes were wide, and her lips parted as if she were about to speak. The sight of Mr. van Kirk presumably gave her pause.

"I am very sorry to bother you," she said soon after

she'd recovered herself. "I wished to speak to Charlotte, but it can wait."

"We were not speaking of anything of importance," Mr. van Kirk said, waving her in. "Come in, come in."

Lucille cautiously entered the room. Her eyes wandered toward shelf after shelf lined with aged spines. Then they darted toward the pot on Mr. van Kirk's desk and the empty chair next to my own.

"Please, sit," Mr. van Kirk invited.

"I really do not mean to impose," Lucille murmured, slowly lowering herself onto the chair. "I wished to see if Charlotte was feeling improved from this morning."

"I am well," I assured her.

"Were you ill?" Mr. van Kirk inquired.

I shook my head.

"Ah, I could not tell for sure," Mr. van Kirk said, turning to Lucille. "Charlotte is exceedingly fond of her gardening. I do not think that even if she were ill she would ever neglect her plants, even when they are dying. She has been this way since she first arrived here."

"Is that so?" Lucille said. "That is an admirable trait."

"You must have seen many a type of flowers since you have been abroad," Mr. van Kirk said. "Have you found any particularly to your liking?"

"Truthfully, I cannot say I paid much attention to the types," Lucille replied. "I only look and enjoy. Have you a favorite from your travels, perhaps?"

"A woman led me to a tulip tree in Calcutta once," he answered immediately, leaning back in his chair and resting his hands on his stomach. "Greenish-yellow flowers with orange on the tips. The leaves were all sorts of shapes—broad, heart-shaped, wedged at the base. The tree bears fruit as well."

I laughed. "That is a tree, though, not a flower. Is this the same woman you have spoken of before?"

Sometimes, when Mr. van Kirk was feeling reminiscent, he spoke of Calcutta: mosques, rare artwork, and people who fascinated him to no end. But what I really wanted to know was if the sky was as gloomy there as it was here. When he breathed, did the aroma of spices overwhelm his nose? Was the food spicy or sweet or sour? In truth, he was never able to answer all my questions.

This time, he didn't laugh. Instead, he insisted, "Oh, but you would enjoy it, Charlotte. I know you would. You could tuck it in your hair, plant it in your ceramic pot, and fill your Wardian case with them. You would find rather quickly that nothing else compares."

"They sound very beautiful," Lucille commented. "I would like to purchase some very much if I am to ever have a home and allowance of my own."

"Yes," Mr. van Kirk said solemnly.

Confused by his change in manner, I could say nothing of the tulip tree that had implanted itself into Mr. van Kirk's memory. Lucille looked nearly as lost at the tone of his voice. I patted Lucille lightly on the hand.

"I am sure you will," I told her.

March 1885

I WATCHED THE SUN SET AND THOUGHT OF GELATIN. THE SKY RESEMBLED THE CAREFULLY MIXED ORANGE OF SUGAR AND FRUIT JUICE hardening above the stovetop. Soon, I thought, the entire sky would darken as if the mold had been overturned and the jelly had turned a muddy red. Eventually, the stars would emerge to overshadow them all.

That morning, Mr. van Kirk had received a letter from his solicitor. I'd collected the mail from Williams and saw the solicitor's seal in the pile, which was unusual because they always conducted business in person. I wanted to see what he'd written, but Mr. van Kirk had taken his breakfast in the library and asked not to be disturbed. Mrs. van Kirk was too preoccupied to bother with the mail, though if she'd let me speak of it, I doubt she'd have turned away news of their accounts.

I only remembered the letter when I spotted a whiff

of smoke floating outside my window. Mr. van Kirk was fond of cigars, but Mrs. van Kirk despised smoke in the house because she said it made her ill. If she caught the slightest hint of it, she refused to leave her bedroom until it faded away.

Pressing my face against the window, I could just make out more smoke floating upward. I couldn't see Mr. van Kirk, but I was sure that he was outside. I made my way down the stairs and outside the manor's front doors.

There I found Mr. van Kirk leaning against one of the ravens with a cigar in his hand. Williams stood off to the side with the passive look on his face that he always wore. He held a box of Mr. van Kirk's cigars in one hand. In the other hand, Williams held a candle, though it was not yet lit.

At the sound of my footsteps, they both turned.

"Ah, Charlotte," Mr. van Kirk said. "It's a fine night to be outside, is it not?"

"Fine indeed," I agreed, letting my eyes wander toward the darkening sky. "Have you received a letter from Jones?"

"Snooping in my mail, are you?" Mr. van Kirk shook his head, but his face was kind. "I have, but it does not concern you."

"I suppose it would be impertinent to ask why."

"It would."

I smiled faintly.

"Why is it, Charlotte, that young people feel the need

to go to Europe?" Mr. van Kirk mused. "I visited myself, but I much preferred India. At least I was quite free to smoke my cigars whenever I wished while I was there."

"It makes no matter for Mrs. van Kirk where you are," I told him. "She will hate it."

"You are right, of course," he chuckled. "Jones is in touch about Victor's spending. Again. What causes a man to dwindle his own fortune, I cannot say. Victor claims its cause is boredom. Are you too frightfully bored, Charlotte?"

"Not at all," I replied.

Mr. van Kirk blew a puff of smoke before chewing on his lip and turning to Williams. "Williams, do you think Charlotte is unhappy?"

Williams stole a glance at me. "I daresay, sir, I do not think she is."

Mr. van Kirk faced me. "I am afraid you might have been lacking in society before Lucille arrived, Charlotte. If that is the case, I apologize."

I began to protest that Mr. van Kirk was ignoring my answer, but Williams interjected. "If I am not overreaching, sir," he said, "I think Charlotte has a propensity to make friends with whomever she meets."

The other turned his head, a half grin on his face. "Lucille is quite taken with her. Has she made a friend out of you too, old man?"

Williams opened his mouth but would not answer.

I couldn't help but grin.

"You know you are very much like a woman I once

knew in Calcutta," Mr. van Kirk told me, inhaling deeply. "You've a familiar spirit about you. A determinedness, toughness. But not too tough, perhaps. Whether this living situation would suit you, I could not be certain. It did not suit her."

I didn't know how I fit this description, but Mr. van Kirk's words had sparked my curiosity. "I've heard you mention her once or twice, but why is she not in the stories you tell?"

"She is in my travel diaries," Mr. van Kirk said. "Williams knows her name."

"I am not sure that I recall," Williams replied stiffly.

Mr. van Kirk pivoted to face him. Williams's face was cast in shadow, but I saw that he had forgotten nothing in the stubborn, stiff way he held himself. Mr. van Kirk clapped him on the shoulder. "Come now, Williams. How long have I known you?"

"Since we were boys," William said automatically. "I have been by your side since the day I was old enough to be."

"We are friends, are we not?"

"Technically, sir—" he began.

Quickly, Mr. van Kirk waved Williams's protest away. "We are friends. You would give your life for me, Williams. And I would do the same for you. Ah, shall I say we are family? Is that a more apt description? Family then."

Williams took a hesitant step forward. "Sir, this sort of talk… Are you sure you're all right?"

Mr. van Kirk bent over and let out a low laugh. The corners of his eyes creased, and he nearly burned a hole in his slacks with the cigar, mindless as he was of it in his hand. Strangely, I found comfort in the sound.

"Forgive me, the both of you, I am getting old and philosophical. That is all," Mr. van Kirk said finally. "I met her a lifetime ago, Charlotte. But she was a marvelous woman."

"I am hardly marvelous, so I cannot be very much like her," I pointed out.

"You have a familiar spirit, Miss Charlotte," Williams put in quietly.

"Familiar, yes," Mr. van Kirk said, inhaling from his cigar once more. "It is to your advantage that your spirit remains familiar, especially after all this marriage business is over."

"You think they'll be wed then?" I asked.

"Yes. You will understand what it all means."

I didn't understand, but there was nothing left to be said on the subject. Mr. van Kirk had put out his cigar and was ready to turn in for the night. He said he'd have to inform Mrs. van Kirk that the solicitor had expressed concerns about the continued increase in expenditures since Victor had returned home. Neither Williams nor I thought Mrs. van Kirk would want to have the conversation at all.

April 1885

WE WERE GATHERED AT THE DINNER TABLE AFTER THE LAST COURSE HAD BEEN SERVED. MR. VAN KIRK SAT AT THE HEAD of the table with Mrs. van Kirk adjacent to him. Lucille sat opposite Mrs. van Kirk with Victor by her side, his hand resting atop hers. I sat next to Mrs. van Kirk, acutely aware that my attention was wanted, but too focused on my lemon sherbet.

The tangy, sweet, and creamy flavor grazed over my tongue. Bright yellow rays burst forth from my lips with every spoonful, lifting my spirits. When Victor cleared his throat once more, I knew that the news would be more bearable if I could continue eating.

Mrs. van Kirk knew what was to come, and she couldn't help but let out a small squeal. I winced. Victor looked mildly annoyed. He cleared his throat again in anticipation of his speech.

"I have something I would like to share with you all,"

he began. "I missed much of the goings-on at Ivywood during my travels, but I look forward to making it my permanent home once more."

Victor paused to glance at Lucille, who blushed.

"I was most fortunate to meet Lucille during this time. And I am even more fortunate to announce that we are to be married."

"Oh!" Mrs. van Kirk shrieked.

She offered her most sincere congratulations to both Victor and Lucille, for which they heartily thanked her. I echoed her sentiments, but I noticed that Mr. van Kirk said nothing. He fixed Victor with an oddly blank look, which Victor didn't miss.

"Well, Father?" Victor prompted. "Will you not congratulate me?"

"Yes," Mr. van Kirk said, picking up his glass from the table and raising it to them. "Congratulations."

The rest of the party missed this uncomfortable exchange. I wondered why Mr. van Kirk was not happier for his son, even as I reminded myself of the lavish circumstances under which Mr. van Kirk had said Victor had gotten himself into financial trouble. Yet Victor's response was to remain stoic about the whole ordeal.

"We will have to have send the announcement to the papers," Mrs. van Kirk said. Her voice grew unbearably high as she began to list the things that needed to be done. "Will your family travel here, Lucille? Shall we have it here or in town? We shall have to invite all of your aunts and uncles, Victor. My son! Getting married."

"Must we concern the papers, Mother?" Victor asked quietly. "We would like to have it very soon."

"Must we concern— Why, I—" Mrs. van Kirk sputtered. "To do otherwise would be scandalous. How soon do you mean?"

I glanced at Lucille. Though her smile had not disappeared, it was tighter now. She directed most of Mrs. van Kirk's questions back to Victor, but added that her parents would need time to make travel arrangements if she and Victor were to have the wedding at Ivywood Manor.

"Yes, but soon," Victor pressed. "Perhaps a month or two from now."

"A month or two?" Mrs. van Kirk said. "People will believe Lucille is with child."

"I would like it to be sooner rather than later," Victor said firmly.

Mr. van Kirk took another sip from his glass, thoughtful. "A month."

Mrs. van Kirk grimaced. Her lips pressed together until they had nearly disappeared in a thin, set line. Then, she became quite determined. "Three months, and even then, we shall need to begin planning right away."

"Oh, you really need not—" Lucille began.

"Tomorrow will have to do," Mrs. van Kirk spoke

over her. "We will have to go over your gown, food, location…everything."

Mrs. van Kirk insisted that I be present when our dressmaker, Mrs. Simpson, arrived at Ivywood's door. Though Mrs. Simpson had been dressing the van Kirks and myself for all the years I'd resided there, I took no pleasure in her visits. Mrs. van Kirk seemed to take fittings as opportunities to criticize my taste in fashion as I recoiled from the most stylish garments.

In this case, however, I knew that Lucille needed a gown to be wed in, and I needed one to attend the ceremony. Mrs. van Kirk also desired a new gown for the occasion, despite Lucille's attempts to convince her that one of the numerous gowns she'd ordered recently would do perfectly well.

Mrs. Simpson was an extraordinarily tall and severe-looking woman. She wore glasses on the top of her head, and her skin was rather pale. Her dress had the silhouette of all the most fashionable garments, but it was made purposefully dull by its lack of color and frills because she was a woman who knew style without excess.

My dress was canary yellow, and I had to discreetly brush the most stubborn remains of dirt from it when I greeted her. I'd gone for a quick ride on Willow prior to breakfasting and hadn't bothered to change into my riding habit. It had rained the night before, and

Willow's hooves had dislodged chunks of mud beneath the green blades and sprayed them about.

"Mrs. Simpson," I said hurriedly.

"Miss Herring." Mrs. Simpson executed a perfect curtsy. "It is always a pleasure."

As we moved toward Lucille's room, Mrs. Simpson proceeded to inquire about the occasion for the new gowns. She grew positively stiff at the prospect of making gowns for such an important occasion, so serious was she about her craft. She didn't have any opportunity to investigate my muddied hem.

Lucille's face scrunched up in confusion at Mrs. Simpson's reaction, but I assured her that it constituted a kindly acceptance of her business. I seated myself on a chair near Lucille's writing desk, while Lucille looked unsure of what to do.

"Now, Miss King, if you'll kindly step over here, I can take your measurements. Miss Herring, if you'll make yourself comfortable. A wedding gown is very serious business. We shall begin right away."

"Certainly," Lucille agreed.

Mrs. Simpson took out a measuring tape and began instructing Lucille. She made her do an elaborate dance—moving, twisting, and turning. Mrs. Simpson's measuring tape encircled Lucille like ribbons streaming from the seamstress's hands. They pranced in silence, with only the sound of Mrs. Simpson's mutterings about the fit to accompany them.

Though Mrs. Simpson's glasses slid down her face

and caught on the bridge of her nose, she paid them no mind. She was too concentrated on fabrics and swathes of frill. And Lucille was an equally thoughtful participant.

"You do not wish to marry, Charlotte?" Lucille inquired after some time.

Mrs. van Kirk had insisted that I take part in the search for a suitor once, but I possessed no inclination to wed. I suppose she'd thought if she tried hard enough, she'd marry me off quickly to an older, wealthy man. But I knew a husband would never allow me to frolic around the estate or mingle with the servants as often as I did. In fact, he would surely reprimand Mr. van Kirk for allowing me to behave so.

"Marriage is a strange institution," I said finally, tapping my knee. "I have never had a strong inclination to marry, as I am very well provided for here. And I am far past the marrying age now."

Lucille tilted her head, and Mrs. Simpson admonished me. "Do you not think it has its advantages?"

"I do believe it has many advantages," I agreed. "Though Mr. van Kirk adopted me, Victor is to inherit the estate. Still, it is not for me."

Lucille pressed her lips together. "I believe it is in my best interest to marry."

"Is that so? I must say, I've begun to think that it is in a lady's best interest to do as she will whenever she wills it. If she wishes to be married, she should do so.

If she does not, then she should not. Do you agree, Mrs. Simpson?"

Mrs. Simpson pouted absentmindedly. "Yes, of course, dear."

The fabrics Mrs. Simpson had laid out consisted of my least favorite things: ruffles and beads. The little round balls were scattered near miscellaneous sewing tools. It took Mrs. Simpson some time to decide on what Lucille's gown needed most.

I felt drained at the sight of it all, but Lucille's face became slightly pink. I couldn't tell if it was from anxiousness or happiness. But she preferred to show concern for me.

"Is something amiss, Charlotte?" she asked.

Mrs. Simpson stopped measuring. She began to gather long pieces of fabric and hold them up in front of Lucille's body. I could see her piecing them together visually with the squint of her eyes.

"Miss Herring does not fancy ruffles," Mrs. Simpson explained, a smile gracing her face for the first time since her entrance. "She does not appreciate the busyness of the higher fashions."

I demurred. "I would not say I dislike it."

Mrs. Simpson said nothing. She pinned the fabric to Lucille, adjusting the waistline and building up the sleeves. The ruffles were added on temporarily, and I tried to control my facial expressions.

"You prefer not to have ruffles on your own gowns," Mrs. Simpson amended.

"But preferences," I continued, "we all know, do not mean much in society. And so I have had several gowns with plenty of ruffles."

"Yes," Mrs. Simpson agreed. "And if I am to have my way, Lucille will have plenty of ruffles on her wedding day as well."

May 1885

THE SOUND OF MR. VAN KIRK AND VICTOR'S RAISED VOICES CREPT THROUGH THE CRACKS BETWEEN THE DOORS OF THE LIBRARY AND the floor. The voices floated down the hall and left short, angry snippets in their wake for others to inadvertently catch. I was planning to retire to my room for the evening when I heard them and slowed my normal stride to a slow creep.

Williams stood outside the door. His face was passive, giving no indication that he could hear the argument taking place within. Only the corners of his mustache twitched, as if trying to escape, when a particularly loud word echoed against the doors.

"Williams," I whispered. "I suppose you will not tell me what they're on about."

He gave me a stern look.

"But it could not possibly be your fault if I chose to

stand next to you, have a chat, and just so happen to overhear," I ventured.

He gave no sign of having heard me at all, so I took that for a yes.

"I am to wed Lucille!" I heard Victor shout.

"This is not news to me," Mr. van Kirk replied, though his voice was much more muffled. "Your lawyer is the same as mine…"

Victor replied, but I couldn't catch what he'd said. Victor's voice was difficult to decipher because it rose and fell with every few syllables. I turned to Williams for help, but he simply shook his head.

"I sincerely hope this is not the reason you have hounded me every night to meet with you. Your mother has already formed plans for your wedding," Mr. van Kirk said.

"It is not. Her dowry—"

"I have had Jones look into her finances. I am aware."

"I can repay you and everyone else on time. That is what I am here to tell you."

"If you were unable to, your credit would have remained questionable here and anywhere else you travel to. You cannot continue on like this."

I turned to Williams. "How large a sum does Victor owe, Williams?"

Williams pursed his lips and glanced around to see if anyone else was coming down the hall. "Perhaps it would be best if you retire to your room now, Miss Charlotte."

"Williams," I pressed.

"Even if I knew, you know as well as I do that it is not my place to say," he responded, looking uncomfortable. "If you wish to take it up with the master, I can certainly inform him of your desire to do so."

I opened my mouth to reply, but Mr. van Kirk's next outburst stopped me.

"I have never raised a son to resort to this sort of devilry to make up for his irresponsibility!"

The words were followed by the sound of glass hitting a table. The *thunk* turned to a slow wobble, as if the glass was rolling around. And then a crash—it must have shattered.

Williams and I looked at each other with wide eyes.

"No, you were too occupied raising another, were you not, Father?"

"If you require something of me, state it clearly, else neither of us will ever know the answer, Victor."

"It makes no matter how I cover my debts."

"You will bring shame upon that poor girl and her family!"

Victor made no reply.

The door to the library swung open, and Williams caught it just before it could hit me in the face. Victor turned on his heel, knocking into Williams, and stomped past us both. Even in his ire, he managed to pause and glare at me. The flecks in his eyes were not brown but black pools, spewing loathsome thoughts in my direction.

I wasn't cold, but I shivered.

Now that the door was open, Mr. van Kirk's voice was much clearer. He called for Williams to put out the fire in the library and clean up the mess Victor had made of their carpet. Williams inclined his head toward me before entering the library, but I didn't move.

"Williams," I heard Mr. van Kirk say. "Have you ever heard my son issue an apology in his life?"

The answer, I knew, was "no." Victor was not the sort of person who apologized for his wrongdoings. And if he ever did so, he made sure you knew that the apology was not sincere with the arc of an eyebrow.

"Never you mind, Williams." Mr. van Kirk sighed. "It was an idiotic question. Of course he has not. Bless the only good child I have."

At this, I dared to peek around the door. Mr. van Kirk was standing by the fire. In one hand, he held the decanter, and in the other, he held two fingers of scotch. I watched him place the decanter down and turn the glass over in his hands multiple times. He lifted it in a mock toast to some invisible person, and though I badly wanted to, I couldn't bring myself to enter.

I TRIED TO SPEAK TO MR. VAN KIRK ON MANY AN occasion about the conversation I'd overheard, but he never seemed to have time for me. He went into town more often than usual, lugging ledgers and papers that I'd never seen before. He spoke to Williams in hushed tones so that none of us could overhear him. One week, he had a slew of visits from Jones. Day after day, Jones entered the library with a serious expression and left with his fashionable coattails swinging behind him.

June 1885

T HE ROOM WAS WARM, TOO WARM TO BE COMFORTABLE. THE SMELL OF STALE SWEAT LINGERED IN THE AIR LIKE A ROTTING carcass. And no breeze swept through the windows to offer us any relief. Not a single leaf brushed against another on any of the foliage. Heedless of everyone's discomfort, Mrs. van Kirk had requested that the servants leave the blinds and curtains open in the drawing room, and we were all suffering for it.

I resisted summoning Williams to ask for someone—anyone, really—to block out some of the light. But I knew that Mrs. van Kirk would protest and complain of all her ailments that the heat could potentially cure. My only source of comfort was that no one looked satisfied with the state of the room except for her and possibly Victor.

Since I'd overheard Mr. van Kirk and Victor's argument, Victor had been in a monstrously good humor. He joked that the temperature resembled what he thought the burning heat in India must be like, constantly looking to Mr. van Kirk for confirmation on the subject. It was the only topic he willingly touched upon when he addressed his father, and the money predicament was never broached in front of the ladies.

"Do you think," Victor said, turning from the window he'd been staring through, "that we could all do with a little more heat? It is like being in the sun."

Mr. van Kirk's face took on a pinched look, but he said nothing.

"Would you agree, Charlotte? You enjoy the sun, do you not?"

I narrowed my eyes. "I suppose I do."

Whatever game Victor was playing was unceremoniously interrupted by Mrs. van Kirk. She brought the subject back to Victor's travels and his and Lucille's upcoming wedding plans. Had Victor been properly fed during his travels? Should they invite her distant cousin twice removed to the festivities?

Victor seemed reluctant to change the subject at first, but he clearly enjoyed his mother's queries about the wedding plans. He smiled and stated that there was no expense too large for them to cover, as if he were simply being kind enough to indulge her. Lucille begged that Mrs. van Kirk refrain from going through too much trouble.

Mrs. van Kirk insisted, "No trouble at all, dear! I

already made arrangements for the church in town. When will my only son ever marry again?"

"You will send invitations to my friends in Europe in addition to the Kings, will you not, Mother?" Victor asked. "And we will have to arrange comfortable accommodations while they are here."

Mr. van Kirk looked pained as his gaze flashed to Lucille's concerned face. He soon changed the subject back to Victor's travels. Victor kept trying to speak of Mr. van Kirk's trip to India instead.

"I would hardly say it is like being in the sun. Not the same experience at all," Mr. van Kirk said in reply to Victor's question about the current weather. "Charlotte would not know any better than you, as neither of you have ever been."

We were all perspiring, but a copious amount of sweat began to drip down Mr. van Kirk's forehead, and his face took on a white pallor. He was squinting, as if trying to prevent the droplets from falling into his eyes. His fingers reached up to tug at his cravat in a vain attempt to loosen it, but Williams had expertly tied it.

Mrs. van Kirk, who was seated across from Mr. van Kirk in a chair of her own, leaned forward. Her nose scrunched up the way one's did when one smelled something particularly nasty. She reached out a concerned hand before letting it fall by her side. "Morton, are you sure you are feeling all right?" she inquired.

Rather than answer, he replied, "It is rather stuffy in here."

I looked at Lucille. She was just as disconcerted as Mrs. van Kirk, except her eyes were resting on the sunlight shining through the windows and the cords and tassels that held the curtains aside.

"I think you best retire," Mrs. van Kirk suggested. "We will ask Williams to ensure that your room is cool and comfortable, shall we?"

"Is it really necessary?" he asked, tugging at every piece of clothing to prevent it from sticking to his skin. "I am just a little overheated."

Mrs. van Kirk rose and pressed her fingers to Mr. van Kirk's forehead. She jumped back as soon as the flesh of her palm met his skin. Her eyes were wide, and she cradled the fingers that had touched him close to her chest.

"Morton, I do believe you have a fever."

Mr. van Kirk shook his head. "How can that be?"

"Have you been feeling unwell?"

"Only since Victor and I—" he began. Then he cleared his throat. "Since a few days ago. I have had much to consider."

Her eyebrows creased. "You best go upstairs."

"Father, I think Mother is right," Victor chimed in rather cheerfully.

Mr. van Kirk looked mutinously at his son. He stood up stock-straight and stomped out. It was clear that he did not appreciate Victor's lively demeanor.

"I think I feel a little lightheaded," I said after he'd left.

"What?" Lucille's voice raised several octaves. "Have you caught it as well?"

"I do believe I am just a little tired," I explained, standing. "You will all excuse me if I retire early, will you?"

"Yes," Mrs. van Kirk agreed. "We should all retire soon."

"Mother is quite right," Victor agreed. "Whatever Father has, we do not want it spreading."

The wedding plans were in full force. Mrs. van Kirk was constantly surrounded by pastel swatches and cream handkerchiefs. She shot up at random, lifted them to eye level to examine them, and then relaxed back into her seat once she was satisfied with her choices. At times, she stained the tips of her fingers with ink from the many to-do lists she'd created for herself. Then she smudged a name while running her fingers over them methodically, and she screeched as if she'd burned her tongue on tea that was too hot for her liking.

If I hadn't known it was Lucille's wedding, I might have thought Mrs. van Kirk was to be wed. Lucille docilely agreed with every word that emitted from Mrs. van Kirk's mouth. The only matter she was concerned with was the arrival of her own family. Lucille insisted upon ensuring the guest bedroom where her parents would be staying was to her standards. She was in constant correspondence with her father in regard to her impending joy. Often, I sat beside her as she penned a letter, crumpled it up, and began anew when she was unable to express herself to her full satisfaction.

Since their engagement, Victor had begun to spend a good deal of his time outside of the manor. He woke very early to visit the gentlemen's club, which he claimed would help boost the family's status, and didn't return until very late at night. Sometimes, he returned in a jolly mood, but more often than not, he was bad-tempered and rude. No one dared ask what had happened, but Mr. van Kirk hinted that Victor had picked up a new vice whenever I asked him.

I thought it odd that Victor wasn't playing a more active role in his wedding plans either, since he had been so insistent about the date, but Mrs. van Kirk shushed me impatiently any time I spoke of it.

Among the chaos, I thought something had been lost. Mr. van Kirk rarely left his bedroom since the heat wave, and he was showing no improvement. I proffered my hand to him whenever I saw him leaning against the stairs, his hand over his heart. He was stubborn and angry, but if I played the more stubborn, he let me walk him to his room. I didn't say a word though, for fear of hurting his pride.

Whenever we reached his destination, he pressed my

hands between his and reiterated that he was perfectly fine, simply stressed. He only released them after I begged him to rest. Then, one day, after Mrs. van Kirk had gone into a frightful fit over the type of cake that would be served, he did something out of character.

He told me, "Charlotte, you needn't fret over me. But do take care of yourself, won't you?"

"Do you fret over me?" I asked, teasing.

He didn't laugh. Instead, he applied light pressure to his temples and mulled it over. "I have reached an age where I think I know death."

"Do we not all know him?"

"We do, but I shall greet him when he comes for me. You are not ready to do that."

I thought about Mr. van Kirk's words endlessly. They nagged at me, pulling at my skirts when my foot touched the staircase or whispering against my hair when there was a light breeze.

He said he knew death, and I came to the conclusion that something was not right in Ivywood Manor, though I could not say what.

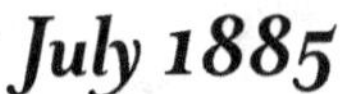 July 1885

IT WAS A GLORIOUS DAY FOR A WEDDING. AT LEAST, THAT'S WHAT MRS. VAN KIRK KEPT REPEATING TO ANY PERSON WHO CAME WITHIN EARSHOT. The clouds were scarce, leaving large blue patches of sky and no sign of rain. The guests were not as quick to praise the weather, but Mrs. van Kirk was taking the sky as an indicator of good fortune for Victor and Lucille's wedded life nonetheless.

I disagreed with this assessment. It rained the entire day prior to the wedding and threatened to continue to rain on the way into town. Upon arrival at the church, the grounds were muddy, so when I stepped with the impact of my full weight, my foot sunk a few centimeters. When I lifted my foot, it came away with chunks of dirt and grass blades. The gathering at the ceremony was not as large as Mrs. van Kirk had hoped it would be. However, she was holding out hope that the reception back at the manor would be larger.

I didn't bother informing Mrs. van Kirk of my observations, as I doubted my opinion would alter hers. The only people who were particularly interested in hearing what I had to say were the servants. They couldn't attend the wedding, as they had to prepare for the feast that followed. Molly and Jack requested a complete account of the ceremony, and I was most happy to oblige.

The ceremony itself was worth talking about at least. Lucille glided down the aisle in an ivory satin gown with a wide, gathered skirt. Her neckline was trimmed by Mrs. Simpson's steady hands into a lace ruffle. The bodice was laced tight over an embroidered chemise and layers of full petticoats. Her mother had given her a guipure lace veil with floral motifs to complete her bridal look, which I admired most. Victor wore a black dress coat with full collar, white vest, and black pantaloons. His suit was pressed neat and wrinkled only slightly when he shifted his weight from one foot to the other as he waited for Lucille to reach his side.

When they said their vows, all who were present wiped the corners of their eyes with embroidered handkerchiefs to avoid the pitfall of looking overcome. I was second to congratulate the happy couple after Mrs. van Kirk, murmuring my most sincere assurances to Lucille. Mr. van Kirk followed me, looking quite grim, and kept his congratulations short. Then we all climbed into carriages to join Victor and Lucille at Ivywood Manor.

The journey back to the manor took time, but it was not without the usual festivities. There were many family members from Mrs. van Kirk's side of the family whom I'd never met. I didn't see many from Mr. van Kirk's side, but this was not unusual. I asked him why we didn't see more of his relatives, and he said they didn't approve of him. At first, I thought he meant Victor, but he clarified that he was speaking about himself; it was most strange.

"Why do they not approve of you?" I asked finally.

Mrs. van Kirk interjected before he could answer, her head held high. "They disliked his choice in partner."

I was so taken by the news that I said nothing at all.

Mrs. van Kirk was many things, but unsuitable wasn't one of them. She came from a decent, well-connected family who had provided her with a large dowry. I'd been told that when she was younger, her beauty rivaled most everyone. There was no reason for Mr. van Kirk's family to object, as far as I knew.

After that, Mrs. van Kirk returned the conversation to the wedding ceremony. She sang the praises of nearly every aspect of it: the gown, the suit, and the way the priest conducted it all. I couldn't help but feel there was an odd tension between Mrs. van Kirk's compliments and Mr. van Kirk's grunts in response.

When we arrived at the manor, the guests were appreciating the well-decorated reception. The tables were covered with expensive cream cloth. Platters of food filled every empty space, the aroma drifting in the air. Baubles were strung up on trees, which reflected sunlight into guests' eyes and made them flinch. I caught myself in a bauble's path more than once that day.

It was festive—the most welcoming scene at the manor yet.

As I stood, taking it in, a distant cousin of Mrs. van Kirk's emerged from the buffet with a glass of champagne. She was clothed in gray moiré taffeta with rose buttons and very wide sleeves lined with white and edged in rose. Her skirt was trimmed with ribbon, and her hair was bound together with rose-colored velvet. She was a vain flower, displaying every petal before it could fall, even more extravagant than Mrs. van Kirk.

"A splendid affair, Dorothea," she complimented. "It's your delicate touch, is it not?"

I turned my back to both Mrs. van Kirk and her cousin. I didn't wish to join their conversation about the baubles or latest fashions. I much preferred standing off to the side, watching Victor reintroduce his bride to every guest who crossed their path.

Lucille was glowing, matching every one of Victor's steps with a glide of her own. Her cheeks were flushed, though it could be due to the plying of champagne upon their arrival at the manor. Her grin was so wide that I thought it couldn't be easily wiped off.

Victor, on the other hand, remained composed. He

was the complete gentleman, shaking hands with every man and bowing to every woman. But he was quick to move from one person to the next.

"The wedding came quickly," I heard her cousin commenting. "I was surprised when I received the announcement."

"Yes, but he has been away for so long," Mrs. van Kirk said.

"You never could deny that boy anything," her cousin replied. "I told you, did I not? I suppose Victor is well off now. She seems a decent girl, good fortune…"

I froze in my spot, unable to ignore their conversation any longer. My eyes slid over to Mrs. van Kirk, who was staring at Mr. van Kirk's back. I thought I saw her eye twitch, but then her gaze ran over me.

She shook her head and returned to her conversation.

"I suppose if they had not found each other, you would have interfered," her cousin stated. "The rumor mill has it that he was near destitu—"

"Do not say that word," Mrs. van Kirk snapped.

The woman hissed. "I did not say you were, Dorothea. Calm yourself. But the boy is no mathematician. These foreign guests alone must have cost you a fortune."

"Yes," Mrs. van Kirk agreed slowly. "But I would have interfered in his finances if I had to."

"Anything for Victor."

"Anything," Mrs. van Kirk repeated. "Absolutely anything."

Victor's plight loomed foremost in my thoughts.

I let the word "destitute" roll around on my tongue, mouthing it with my lips but refusing to form the sound. The taste was bitter, and I wondered if Lucille tasted the same thing. She had entered their marriage knowing her fortune would no longer be hers, but she hadn't protested. Would she endure destitution for Victor now that they were wedded in such an extravagant fashion and on their way to their costly nuptial journey? I didn't know.

Part II

September 1885

IVYWOOD MANOR FELT CHANGED AFTER VICTOR AND LUCILLE'S WEDDING. THE COUPLE HAD TRAVELED TO VENICE WHEN THE CELEBRATION was over and planned to return in a few weeks' time. Mr. van Kirk was grim again, as if the details of the wedding and nuptial journey had inflamed his health issues once more. He adamantly refused to see a doctor. Mrs. van Kirk was nearly as upsetting to be around. She felt the loss of her son more keenly now that he was married than ever before. She snapped at the servants, who approached her more frequently than they had when Victor was absent due to school or his travels.

I found that the most fitting solution to avoid general despair was to spend my free time away from others. I stood in the guest room in front of my Wardian case, removing old ferns and ivy that I'd once kept. I added new pots of herbs for Molly's kitchen as I had promised

I would, arranging and rearranging them as I planted seeds and monitored their progress.

If I was not in the guest room, I stayed in the library. It was unfortunate that prior to the trip to Venice, Victor had ventured into the space so often. He'd made it different by shelving books haphazardly: he never returned them to the spot he'd found them, left them on their covers between shelves, and damaged the corners by placing them at odd angles. But more importantly, he'd altered the smell of the room. The aged leaflets and ink blots were overpowered by Victor's cologne—a musky, almost wild smell that I'd tried to erase.

I enlisted Jane's help to rearrange the books into their proper order. We dusted shelves and ordered stray papers into neat stacks. Occasionally, Mr. van Kirk, who alternated between staying in his room and the library, was there too. He made no mention of our efforts to restore the library to its usual order, but his shoulders visibly relaxed as we made progress in the organization.

"Am I allowed to enter?" he called from the doorway one day.

I replied, "Most certainly."

Instead of seating himself behind his desk, he settled into the chair on the opposite side. He picked up one of the books, furrowed his eyebrows, and rested his hand on the cover as if marking it for later perusal. He called to me without urgency to sit and talk with him.

I seated myself hesitantly in his chair.

"Have you been well?" he asked.

I repeated the question back to him.

"I have not been my usual self, it is true," he admitted. "But it comes with old age. You would not torture an old man by dodging his concerns, would you?"

I answered, sullen. "I have been well enough."

"You seem changed since Victor's wedding," he observed. "But I suppose we all have been changed in one way or another."

My fingers fluttered over the book Mr. van Kirk had eyed earlier, stalling. "I overheard a bit of a conversation."

"A conversation?" he prompted.

"Yes."

"And it has upset you?"

"I would not say that. I have been getting along perfectly fine. I have only thought about it a few times since I heard it."

"But it has upset you," he said.

"Sir," I began, hesitant. "A woman said some things… She spoke of Victor's finances, and Lucille's in turn."

"Ah." He picked up the ledger and turned it over in his hands. Spotting a gathering of dust, he blew it clean. The dust floated in the air for a moment before settling on top of the desk. "Is that all?"

"Well, yes," I replied. "I am under no illusion that they married for love, and I am sure the marriage settlement was fair. But I worry for Lucille, that is all."

Mr. van Kirk formed a steeple with his fingers beneath his chin. "Victor and Lucille's marriage was settled upon together, and the way in which they conduct themselves now is entirely up to them."

"I suspected as much," I sighed.

"You care for Lucille greatly, and she cares for you."

"Yes," I confirmed.

"Trust that she knows what she's doing."

I ran my finger over the spine of the ledger. "It is Victor who I do not trust."

"That is true."

"So how can I trust that she will be okay?"

As he opened his mouth to reply, he fell into a coughing fit. He clutched at his chest and hacked for several prolonged seconds. I rose from my seat, reaching out a hand to help, but I knew that there was nothing I could do for him. Finally, when the coughing had subsided, I told him I'd send for a doctor.

"No!" he protested. Then, more quietly, "Send for Williams."

I was not pleased with his request. I very much respected Williams, and he had stood by many of our bedsides during colds, but he was not a doctor. Yet I couldn't refute Mr. van Kirk's request, and I rang the bell.

I KEPT A WATCHFUL EYE ON MR. VAN KIRK AFTER that. Prior to the wedding, he was unwell, but I'd thought he'd shown improvement. I was clearly wrong. He often cleared his throat or laid a hand over his chest and took deep, slow breaths as if he couldn't get enough air into his lungs. And he was tired, slower in his movements.

It could've been an ache in the head or old age for all I knew. But now I thought it boded ill.

October 1885

THE FAMILY WAS GATHERED IN THE INFORMAL DRAWING ROOM TO PREPARE FOR VICTOR AND LUCILLE'S RETURN FROM VENICE. MRS. VAN Kirk sat on the edge of a chair with her legs crossed, a look of concentration on her face. Mr. van Kirk and I sat on the settee—him half listening to her suggestions and me thumbing through a poetry book.

When Mr. van Kirk first sat down, he suggested that his account of the world was far more poetic. I replied that I sincerely hoped he was right, and he said perhaps he'd show me his travel diaries, particularly the one from India, one day. The mention of them sparked my interest, but Mrs. van Kirk, completely unaware of the contents of our conversation, impatiently interrupted us.

"I think it best if we have a dinner," she said. "I want every course to be absolutely stunning."

"Is it necessary to make such a fuss?" I asked.

"It is a splendid idea, really. I do not see why Molly

cannot prepare something special for them. My only son does not get married every day," she continued.

"He is already married," Mr. van Kirk amended.

I pressed my lips together and flipped back to the first page of the book.

Mrs. van Kirk huffed. "Well, return from his nuptial journeys then. It cannot be extraordinarily difficult to make a little more food than usual."

"Victor and Lucille have surely had their fill of wedded bliss. And it might be…less than ideal for Molly to attempt to outdo herself on such short notice," Mr. van Kirk explained.

Mrs. van Kirk opened her mouth to protest, then closed it. She tapped her fingers against the table, scanning the list in front of her. I couldn't read her thin, tall letters from this angle, but I imagined that everything on the list was too important to her to put aside in favor of another's suggestions.

"Perhaps," she said grudgingly.

Mrs. van Kirk uncrossed her legs, rang for Williams, and sat down again. The movement of her finger against her temple drew my eye. She drummed incessantly, and I pictured her tapping a key on the pianoforte—only the one—but expecting to hear a different sound each time.

When Williams arrived, Mrs. van Kirk said, "Will you ask Molly to prepare something special for Victor's return?"

"Yes, my lady," Williams said. "Anything in particular?"

"Cream of asparagus soup, light salad, baked salmon… Roast chicken with potato, do you think, dear?" She turned to Mr. van Kirk but didn't wait for his answer. "Ham timbales, as well. Cucumber sauce, green peas, mousse au chocolate. Maybe a few pastries, and coffee most certainly—"

"Dorothea," Mr. van Kirk called, stopping her. "That is quite enough to do, do you not think?"

Her face turned slowly toward Mr. van Kirk, as if she were a fragile doll whose neck could only twist so far in the opposite direction. The strings would wear down with each added degree, stretching and thinning sinews, until there was nothing to hold her parts together. I pictured the ravens reaching her, swooping down and circling her disjoined body.

Williams asked, "Will that be all?"

Mr. van Kirk didn't let his wife speak. "Yes, thank you, Williams. That will be all."

Mrs. van Kirk's left eye twitched, but she said nothing. She angled her body away from her husband and put all her effort into listing the dishes she'd requested from Molly. Occasionally, I thought I heard her murmur softly, testing which words felt the most appropriate to greet her son with.

"THEY'LL BE HERE ANY MOMENT—ANY MOMENT!"

Mrs. van Kirk repeated those words like a mantra. She bustled around the manor, checking and double-checking that everything was to her liking. Were the rooms readied? Had the preparation for dinner begun? Did the servants know that Victor and Lucille weren't to be bothered in case they were tired from their journey?

I grew bored of hearing Mrs. van Kirk's shrill voice doling out instructions. The words jumbled together so that they made no sense unless you had a practiced ear. I almost wondered how her voice traveled so far in a manor as large as Ivywood. But then again, she meant to be heard.

When Jane came to fetch me from my bedroom because Mrs. van Kirk had spotted Victor and Lucille's carriage near the gates, I was relieved. Mrs. van Kirk could redirect her attention to Victor rather than the servants. Jane followed me out of my room, down the stairs, and to the front door, where Williams stood ready to greet the couple.

I was surprised Mrs. van Kirk was not by his side yet.

"Hello, Williams," I said. "Have you been assigned the task of greeting Victor and Lucille as well?"

His response was immediate. "I am more than happy to do so, Miss Charlotte."

"Right," I muttered.

He gave me a sardonic look.

Beyond the door, I heard voices whispering. Their words overlapped one another in quick bursts. I could clearly make out Victor's voice rising in order to get the last word with a particularly curt, "Enough." From the corner of my eye, I saw Williams's eyes widen slightly, betraying his surprise.

Nonetheless, he opened the door.

Victor and Lucille looked much changed since their wedding day. Victor's lanky figure was clothed in a dark blue suit, and his face was impassive. But he stared at Williams as if he could see through him and the walls, too. The change in Lucille was more apparent. Her hair was a little unkempt, and there was a noticeable crease in her skirts where her hands gripped it too tightly, though she smiled.

"Charlotte," Lucille breathed.

She released her skirts, walked toward me quickly, and grasped both of my hands tight in hers. She squeezed, and I thought I saw the ghost of a tear in her eye. Was I mistaken?

"It is so good to see you," she murmured.

I squeezed her hands back. "And you as well."

She stepped aside, and I thought to greet Victor. But Mr. and Mrs. van Kirk swept into the room. Victor's eyes flashed at Mrs. van Kirk's outstretched embrace, and her arms twitched in response. She let them fall reluctantly as she approached Victor, while Mr. van Kirk kept his distance.

"Victor," Mrs. van Kirk sighed.

Victor leaned forward to give Mrs. van Kirk a chaste kiss on the cheek. Partially contented by her son's touch, she told Williams to have someone bring their trunks to their rooms. Then she asked if there were any troubles with the journey home.

"No, but I am fatigued," Victor announced, heading to the staircase. "May we speak of this at dinner?"

Mrs. van Kirk was taken aback. "I thought we might—"

"You have not changed the dinner hour, I am certain?" Victor said, raising his eyebrows. "You can wait a few hours to hear from us."

"Lucille," Mr. van Kirk said. "Would you like to rest as well?"

"I—" she began.

"She will rest, too," Victor decided.

Lucille looked uncomfortable, stuttering, "I—I would rather not."

Victor stopped at the bottom of the staircase, his fingers gripping the banister. His shoulders tensed briefly before he faced us. His expression was blank when he informed Lucille that she could certainly do whatever she wished, no matter how willful she might seem doing so.

Lucille cast her eyes downward.

"We are glad to see you," I said, directing my words at Victor. "But perhaps it would be best if you rested. Refreshed yourself."

He threw his head back and chuckled. "Ah, I will. You are kind to think of my health, Charlotte. But like Lucille, I will do as I wish."

Victor climbed the stairs quickly, leaving a silent

room in his wake. Lucille wasn't quite normal, and she couldn't seem to bring herself to move either here nor there. Mrs. van Kirk was monstrously upset at me for provoking Victor when he clearly said he wanted rest; I knew this because she hissed the words in my ear. The only thing Mr. van Kirk had to say was, "Welcome home, Lucille." Then he sat down, exhausted by the exchange.

Dinner was quite the display. Molly delivered on every dish that Mrs. van Kirk had requested. The asparagus soup was delightful, the salmon and chicken done to perfection, the ham honey-laden, and the mousse au chocolate sweet. I focused most of my attention on dining because Victor and Lucille were stiff as a board throughout, no matter what question Mrs. van Kirk posed.

"Are you certain you are feeling quite well, Lucille?" Mr. van Kirk asked finally.

Lucille patted the corners of her lips with her napkin. "Thank you for your concern. I was only feeling a little faint, but I am sure I am already much improved. It is so nice to see you all."

"She is fine, Father," Victor said.

Mr. van Kirk's eyes narrowed slightly. "Yes, I heard her say so."

"Oh! It is yourself you should be worrying over," Mrs.

van Kirk said, her voice higher than usual. "Your father has not been well, Victor."

Mr. van Kirk stiffened. "Hold your tongue, Dorothea."

She turned to Victor. "Stays all day in that library of his. Retires early to bed. Does not even touch his cigars now, does he?"

"Dorothea," he repeated more forcefully.

She countered. "It is not as if I am telling lies."

At this, Victor perked up. He leaned forward so that his body was facing Mr. van Kirk. His brown eyes were wide, and his pale lips parted. The look reminded me of Victor as a young lad, laughing in excitement as Mrs. van Kirk approached me with her finger wagging in the air.

"Is it true? You are unwell, Father?" he asked.

"I am well enough," Mr. van Kirk replied curtly. "Your mother frets needlessly. It is not for you to worry about."

Victor leaned back, appearing concerned. "But I am worried, Father. I know how you like your affairs to be in order—on all accounts."

"Indeed," Mr. van Kirk replied. "I do, and they are."

I highly doubted that Victor could say the same, especially since they had planned to meet some of his wealthier companions in Venice. Victor gave such a scathing look to Mr. van Kirk that I couldn't help but blurt out, "Are yours?"

"Charlotte!" Mrs. van Kirk reprimanded. Then she let out a nervous giggle. "Let us speak of pleasanter topics, Victor. You and Lucille have only come home today, and I do not wish the day to be spoiled by this sort of talk."

Victor didn't reply. Instead, he ran his fingers over the tablecloth in front of him, tracing the swirling patterns. By the time he removed his hand, the cloth had gathered into a small clump. He raised his head, and I refused to let my gaze wander away; he met my eyes unflinchingly.

"I want what is best for this family, Charlotte. I am to take charge of this household. But I should not expect you to understand."

I bit my lip—hard. I didn't see why Victor felt the need to remind me that I was without a role in this family, and, as far as I knew, I was not to inherit much more than a woman of my station could expect.

"Victor," Lucille cautioned, covering his hand with her own. "You need not say anything more."

Mrs. van Kirk laughed and said that Victor meant no harm. He was simply pointing out the facts. And though Mr. van Kirk didn't openly support one side or the other, he gave me a short nod that said it was best for me to remain docile, like a caged animal anticipating the day I would finally be released.

November 1885

GRAY, FOGGY CLOUDS MADE FOR AN OMINOUS SKY FROM THE HORIZON TO RIGHT IN FRONT OF MY HANDS. THE WIND BLEW STEADY AND strong, rocking tree branches and tousling horses' manes. Leaves were strewn across the grounds, and flower petals separated from their yellowing stems. It was a gloomy day, though not as gloomy as it would've seemed had it begun to rain.

I intended to take my mare, Willow, out for a trot around the estate, but when I arrived at the stables, Charles quickly disillusioned me of that idea. Willow was not quite herself, and I wondered whether it was the weather that had gotten to her. Charles said that he'd no doubt Willow would be much better to ride on the morrow, so I stroked Willow's mane and retreated indoors.

I entered the informal drawing room, only to discover the handsomely furnished room dimmer than usual. The round table was without its usual shine, the draperies around the piano legs looked faded, and the writing desk was completely bare. I'd read all my correspondence, and I was left with nothing to answer.

Victor and Lucille had gone into town to settle some business, of which Victor refused to speak. Mrs. van Kirk insisted upon joining them, leaving Mr. van Kirk happily without her company. It occurred to me that Jane and I were equally bored by the prospect of wandering around the empty manor, as I'd always thought Ivywood was at its best when there were people to inhabit it and enjoy all the charms it offered.

"Shall we pay a visit to the kitchen, Jane?" I asked.

Jane had begun her needlework, but my suggestion gave her pause. She didn't have some of the other servants' strict perspective on flouting the rules of society, but she was hesitant. I liked the response no better now than I had when I was younger.

"Do you require something from the kitchen, Miss Charlotte?" Jane inquired. "I can send for it right away if that is the case."

"Not at all the point," I countered, rising to my feet. "I will just nip in for a bit. It will be as if I never left."

"Ah, Miss Charlotte!" Jane protested.

But I was already heading in that direction. I hitched my skirts so that I wouldn't slip in my rush and half skipped down the hall. The wall hangings with the stoic faces that decorated them—a stern-looking woman's eyebrows slanted down, a man's nose turned up, and another man's lips pursed together into a thin line much like Victor's—stared down at me in disapproval.

"Miss Charlotte!" Jane called again.

I paused. "Jane, how unusual it is for you to be so reluctant to visit Molly? Have you gotten into a tiff of some sort with her? Because I think—"

"No!" Jane shook her head vehemently. "We have no tiff with each other. It is…well, the young master, Miss Charlotte."

"Victor?"

Jane mumbled something under her breath before sighing. "Yes, Miss Charlotte. I am afraid that he has been saying some unspeakable things about the time you spend with the servants."

"Unspeakable?"

"Insulting and unspeakable," she clarified, sheepish. "He says he does not approve of your habits. You will…further lower your station. I do not want to give him another reason to talk, miss."

"Is that true?" I asked.

She nodded.

Decidedly, I glanced at the doors to the kitchen and then pushed through. Molly was not in the kitchen; in fact, no one appeared to be there. I was forced to head to the servants' quarters, where they typically dined, in search of her.

There, to my surprise, was Williams sitting at the end of the table with a letter in his hand. He jumped at the sight of me and scrambled to his feet to give me a low, unusually clumsy bow. I noticed that his coat was slightly atilt, and his eyes were wide.

"Miss Charlotte," he greeted me.

"I do apologize. I did not mean to disturb you, only Molly was not in the kitchen," I murmured.

Williams clutched the letter in his hand more tightly, and I saw the corner of Mr. van Kirk's seal—a hunched red raven—peeking from behind his fingers. He laid them on the table, straightened his suit, and gestured to a seat for me to sit in. But I politely declined as his eyes wandered to Jane in curiosity.

"Are you in need of anything, Miss Charlotte?" he asked.

"Not particularly," I admitted.

"Molly and the others have gone to town to pick up some flour and spices," he explained, gesturing toward the kitchen. "They should be back any moment now."

"Oh," I said, scrunching up my nose in thought. "Is it Tuesday already? I have lost count of the days."

"Yes, Miss Charlotte," he informed me. "But if you should want for anything, I am perfectly capable of making it for you."

"Truthfully, I only wanted to say hello," I answered, as heat began to flush my face. "I have not had the opportunity to see her recently."

Williams nodded in understanding. "I can make you some tea, if you desire it."

"Perhaps I could do with a cup," I agreed. "Molly taught me to make one for myself, remember? Mrs.

van Kirk was furious when she found out that I was spending time in the kitchen."

Williams tilted his head, regarding me closely. "Yes, I recall."

I glanced at Jane. "Do you think I spend too much time with you all, Williams?"

"You are very kind to pay your servants a visit," he answered slowly. "It is unusual to do so in other households, but I am sure you are aware of that."

"Yes, but would you fault me for caring for you, Williams? I know some people do, but we are family," I said. "It is only that Victor feels—"

"Yes, I am aware of the situation, Miss Charlotte," he said, "and I cannot fault you for anything, especially not for your kindness. You are very much like someone else in that regard."

Every feature of his face began to soften, and I knew he meant Mr. van Kirk. I was reminded of the very first time I asked his name. He was looking at me as if I were nine, too, but I was no longer hiding behind Mr. van Kirk's coattails.

December 1885

"Charlotte, should you be fiddling with Molly's plants?"

I turned, mid-inspection of the herbs, to find Lucille standing in the doorway of the guest bedroom. I must've left it ajar when I entered. She was standing in a ruffled gown with her hands on her hips, as if she were trying to look stern.

Per Molly's request, I'd recently added cilantro, basil, dill, and mint to the collection of herbs in the Wardian case. Mint, in particular, was a favorite of mine. I was pleased to find that they were all thriving within their glass confinement, and I checked on them frequently.

"If you are concerned about Molly, I suggest you don't touch the plants either," I warned.

Lucille paused, appearing to ponder the idea of Molly scolding her. The corner of her lip twitched before she broke into a grin. Then she let out a short laugh and walked toward me.

"I would not dream of doing so," she admitted.

She extended her arm and urged me to hook mine with hers. Her hand brushed against my own as our arms intertwined, and I knew her mood was much improved from the other day.

"Are you in wedded bliss?" I inquired, disentangling myself from her in order to shift the pot of basil a little to the left.

Lucille peered inside but avoided answering my question. "Should we water them?"

"As they are mine, not Molly's, I think we should. But I'm harvesting some for her first, and then I'll bring it to the kitchen for her. Would you like to help?"

Lucille nodded.

Together, we picked off the leaves from the different herbs in silence. I ran my thumb and index finger down the length of the stems, and she imitated my actions. When we had picked a sufficient amount from each ready herb, I gestured for her to follow me.

"Should we be simply waltzing in?" she asked as we walked down the stairs and through the hall.

I lifted my shoulders and let them fall again after a beat. "If you ask Mrs. van Kirk, she will say no, we most certainly should not waltz in. But if we wish to save Molly the effort of harvesting herbs herself, she will certainly allow it."

Lucille nodded.

I led her through the doors and into the kitchen. We said good morning to Molly and the other cooks.

Lucille handed the fresh herbs to Molly, who said she greatly appreciated it. When asked where we were headed off to, I answered that we had to replace all the ones we'd picked off. Lucille laughed as we made our way back to the guest room again.

After picking the stems of some of the herbs bare, the case looked a tad untidy. Patches of dirt speckled the leaves of the remaining herbs. I shifted the pots around, reminding myself to acquire more thyme soon. At least the amount of plants we had now was sufficient for Molly's needs.

Lucille peered closely at the dill. "May I ask, why do you tend to the herbs? I was under the impression that your interest was in flowers."

"I like to see how everything grows, not only flowers."

"Knowing what you're consuming, I suppose."

I nodded. "Truly, though, how is married life? Have you received bundles of letters of congratulations from distant relatives whom you cannot recall?"

She smiled wryly. "It is rather ordinary, actually. Victor and I spent a few days together, but he comes and goes. He is often at the gentlemen's club."

"Ah, so you have not had the opportunity to meet people who marvel at your married state, as I do?"

A small laugh burst from Lucille's lips. "On the contrary, I have received many callers and letters of congratulations. But I have greeted many of them quite alone."

I plucked a wilting basil leaf and brought it to

my nose—it smelled like pepper, almost minty. The robustness of it made me draw my hand away. I offered it to Lucille, and she took a halfhearted sniff, wrinkling her nose.

"Hearty," she commented. "Charlotte, there is no need for you to answer this, of course, but I wondered ..."

I made a humming sound to show I was listening as I prodded at the dirt in the pots to see if it needed watering.

"Victor has told me that you were adopted," she continued. "And I wondered whether you knew what happened to your parents?"

I straightened. "My parents? I have not a clue."

"Have you never wondered though?" she pressed. Then, sighing, "Oh, I do apologize. It is very insensitive of me."

"You're not insensitive," I assured her. "I am curious, of course. But the woman at the orphanage, Nancy, never told me much. If anyone knew, she would've."

Lucille repeated Nancy's name, letting the sound of it roll over her tongue as if she were trying to familiarize herself with every syllable.

"The van Kirks have welcomed me into their home," I continued, "and it seemed ungrateful to ask, though I have in the past to no avail."

When I first arrived at Ivywood Manor, there were many times that I asked Mr. van Kirk questions about my adoption. Since they had my last name, didn't they know the name of my birth mother? Why did she take me to the orphanage? I was certain that the information would have been provided to him upon my adoption, but he said he knew no more than I did.

Over time, I grew to accept that I would never know.

Lucille nodded slowly and said, "I see."

"Is there a reason you ask?"

She hesitated. "Victor gives the impression that he knows something. I have not asked him directly, of course."

"Is that so?" I murmured.

"I do not want to anger him."

"I have noticed that he is especially angry upon returning from town," I pressed. "Does he grow angry often then?"

She didn't answer.

We spent a few more minutes in the guest room as I watered the plants that needed it. I told Lucille how the layout worked and encouraged her to feel leaves here and there. She remained distracted for the rest of the time, though, so I said that it was time for me to wash up.

She relaxed at my suggestion, the tension draining from her face. I, however, went to my room, stared at the dirt in my fingernails and the color of my hands, and felt tenser than ever. I didn't know what Victor knew about my birth parents, but I wanted to.

Later that night, I reclined near my windowsill with Jane by my side. I'd procured a smaller ceramic pot in which I planted tip cuttings from the *Abutilon striatum*. Most people referred to it as the parlor maple, but as I neither kept it in the parlor nor did it resemble maple in its current state, I preferred its scientific name. Jane watched as I tended to it, ready to assist me.

I held my notes in which I'd recorded the day I'd planted the *Abutilon striatum*, their progress, and the days they wilted and died. It was Williams who'd suggested the idea after I'd replanted the cuttings from the once healthy blossoms. Now, I'd resolved to wait.

Soon, the leaves would sprout light green and contain hints of gold. The petals would form a bell shape, colored salmon, white, and yellow. They would range, almost wild unless I pinched the tops of the branches. I had yet to determine whether I would ensure their compactness.

"They will grow, Miss Charlotte."

"You think, Jane? These have been such a challenge."

"You take such care with them."

While I did my best to monitor the cuttings, my mind was elsewhere. I thought of Victor's visits to the club and his resulting angry behavior, Lucille's frightened tone when she spoke of Victor and my own family, and Mr. van Kirk's lingering illness. Everyone in the family appeared to me with heads drooping like leaves and arms moving restlessly like petals falling off a flower. Yet I couldn't reconcile the idea that I was at the pollen-filled center of it all.

January 1886

THE STATE OF THE INHABITANTS OF THE MANOR HAD WORSENED. MR. VAN KIRK'S CONDITION CONTINUED TO SHOW NO improvement, Mrs. van Kirk holed herself up in her chambers, Victor spent all his time in the library, and Lucille hardly spoke at all. I sat at my writing desk, absorbed in the ink and books laid out before me.

After several days of my insisting, Mr. van Kirk allowed me to call upon the family doctor. The doctor paid several visits, made suggestions to keep the room closed tight, and said not to have visitors stomping in and out the doors. But he couldn't pinpoint the illness or its timeline, which vexed me greatly.

Heedless of the doctor's orders, I visited Mr. van Kirk at least twice a day. He spoke very little to me, but I thought he enjoyed the visits even so. I spoke to him about my plans for new flowers or a new book I'd read, but all the while, I thought of Mr. van Kirk claiming he knew death, or Victor telling Lucille he knew something about my birth parents.

Still, I couldn't bring myself to ask about either.

Mr. van Kirk had taken me in when I had no one else. He'd given me an education, loaned me his books, and cared for me. If I could do nothing else for Mr. van Kirk, I would not distress him while he was ill. Instead, I would take matters into my own hands.

Determined, I made my way to the informal drawing room with notebook tucked under my arm. I don't know why I took it with me. I only knew that I didn't wish to leave it unattended. Jane, amazed at the change in my disposition, trailed after me.

"Miss, do you require something?" Jane asked, lightly placing a hand on my shoulder.

"I do not," I replied. "I am feeling splendid, Jane. Well, I am feeling rather piqued, actually. I would very much like to accomplish a few things, and I do not think I can do it on an empty stomach."

In the informal drawing room, I found Lucille sitting on the settee. Her needlework was in her lap, and she looked very surprised when I seated myself beside her. Then I got up again to ring for Williams to bring up the tea tray.

"Oh, Miss Charlotte, I could have fetched you your tea," Jane said.

"Do not be silly, Jane," I countered. "I have already rung for it."

Lucille fiddled with the work in her hands.

"Charlotte! You look well. Have you come to join me for a spot of tea?"

I leaned forward to get a closer look at Lucille's design. Her lines were straight and clean, much unlike my own if I were to try. I shook my head, knowing that it was best if I stuck to my books.

"I have a theory," I announced.

"Theory?" she repeated.

"A theory," I said again. "About Mr. van Kirk. What if his illness is not physical at all? What if it is mental?"

"Mental," she deadpanned. "Charlotte, the doctor said—"

"The doctor has not said anything at all," I interrupted, waving my hand in the direction of Mr. van Kirk's room. "He has said to keep everything closed, but he has not the faintest idea what is wrong! What if Mr. van Kirk is troubled? Deeply."

"Dee—"

"Oh! Lucille, please do stop repeating every word I say. Deeply troubled, yes! And Victor…"

Lucille flinched at the sound of his name.

I hesitated. "Victor, you said so yourself, seems to know something. Or many things. But Mr. van Kirk knows many things too. About Victor."

"You make no sense, Charlotte!" Lucille protested.

I turned to Jane, pleading with her to understand. She, however, remained near the door with her hands behind her back. Her face gave away nothing.

"Does Victor know my birth parents, Lucille?" I asked.

She shook her head vehemently. "I know nothing. I did not know what I was speaking of the day I asked you about them."

I opened my mouth to counter her statement, but Williams entered the room. He laid the tea tray down on the table in front of us and asked if there was anything else either of us required. Both of us thanked Williams but asked for nothing more.

"You do know, Lucille," I said finally. "And you know something is amiss with Victor."

She shook her head vehemently. "I have already told you I do not."

"I do not believe the Lucille I first met would not have told me."

Lucille stood and exited the room. But not before saying, "It is not fair to ask that of me. Victor is my husband."

"Yes, and I am your friend," I murmured.

Mr. van Kirk's room smelled like that of a dead man. The windows were closed tight, and the doors were kept shut. He grew so used to this that he complained of a cold draft whenever someone entered the room. His body ached and shivered; other times, he sweated so heavily that his sheets were drenched and had to be changed.

His temperature rose, fell, and then rose again. The fever wouldn't disappear, no matter how many cool cloths Williams laid over his body. He coughed, too. It started with a dry rasp that made it sound as if he were gasping for breath. Then it moved on to a mucus-filled hacking. Most recently, blood began to stain his white embroidered handkerchief.

To move pained him, and he spoke sparingly. I had to put my ear almost on top of Mr. van Kirk's lips now in order to hear him, but he made no sense. He asked for a woman named "Marjory" and spoke of tulip trees. I thought she must have been the woman from Calcutta, but I said nothing of it to anyone.

"Jones," he rasped.

"Jones?" I repeated blandly. "You want to see Jones?"

He took a long, unsteady breath, and said, "*You* want to see Jones."

I took Mr. van Kirk's hands in my own. "I do not understand. Why would I see Jones? He handles all your affairs. Victor said you have taken care of your property well. I know of nothing else that needs to be done."

"See Jones soon," he instructed, shaking his head. "With Williams."

I contemplated seeing the family lawyer with only Williams, but I could not see why he would play an essential role. I asked Mr. van Kirk if he wished to see anyone else—Mrs. van Kirk? Victor? Maybe Lucille?

But he shook his head to indicate that he preferred his peace and quiet.

When the doctor came in, Mr. van Kirk made no effort to resist his probing and prodding. The doctor pronounced that Mr. van Kirk must have worsened considerably and brought Mrs. van Kirk in to inform her.

She strode into the room in a laurel-green day gown, her head held high. The doctor politely asked her to sit, but she refused. Instead, she stood on the opposite end of the bed and stared down at her husband's sleeping form.

"It will not be long now," the doctor said.

Mrs. van Kirk lifted her eyes to meet my own and stood stock-still. After a moment, she averted her gaze from Mr. van Kirk and myself. She thanked the doctor for all his hard work and asked if there were any other steps that needed to be taken.

"Make him comfortable," the doctor replied. "If there is anything that I can do to make this better…?"

"There is not," she snapped. "He will die, and I will soon be a widow."

"Of course. I apologize for asking."

"This room smells atrocious. Williams should clean it better."

"Ah," the doctor began. "I have asked that we let as few people in and out of the room as possible, and only when necessary."

"It is his job," she said flatly.

"He does a fine job," I countered. "You should not criticize him for the state of the room."

She sniffed at me.

I debated retorting, but I thought I saw tears in her eyes as she left the chamber.

Victor made his first visit in days to Mr. van Kirk after the family had dined. He stood, much like Mrs. van Kirk, ramrod straight on the side of Mr. van Kirk, but he had not the courage to touch him. Mrs. van Kirk shuttered herself in the darkest corner of the room, far from her husband's view. Lucille was relatively composed. She alternated between fluffing Mr. van Kirk's pillow and standing by Victor's side.

"How long?" Victor asked.

Williams's face was scrunched up with concentration. He wrung out a dirty cloth in order to place another on Mr. van Kirk's forehead. Mr. van Kirk's eyes were closed, but his breath was faint. He didn't even flinch when his butler's hands lingered over his forehead.

"Williams," Victor snapped. "I said, how long?"

Pulled out of his stupor, Williams stepped away from the bed and bowed. He looked more confused than ever at Victor's short temper. I took a step forward to pat Williams on the back.

"My apologies, sir," Williams said. "The doctor said it could be anytime."

"Well, what the deuce are you doing changing cloths if he is about to die? Leave him be!"

Williams took a step back, and for the first time I saw that he'd lost the composure he so prided himself upon. He was not the stern butler who refused to give me his name when I was nine. Instead, he was a man desperately doing everything in his power to cure another's ailment.

"I am very sorry if I have offended you, sir," Williams said quietly. "It was not my intention. I only meant to help."

"Victor!" Lucille admonished. "Really."

Victor's face screwed up in scorn. "Do you insist on staying here out of guilt, Williams? You've killed him, haven't you?"

Lucille gasped. "What are you implying?"

"I imply nothing. Williams could not stand the high position I—no, my father—occupied in life. Moreover, he couldn't stand his own position, could he? It is murder, I say."

Mrs. van Kirk began to sob. Lucille gripped Victor's arm in a vain attempt to restrain his words, while I stood there helpless. I wrapped my hands around one of Williams's arms as fat tears rolled down his cheeks and his back hunched over in resignation.

"I apologize," he mumbled. "I apologize, Miss Charlotte."

I glared at Victor before turning back to Williams and making shushing sounds. "You stay right here,

Williams. You did not kill him. You would not hurt a fly."

"I would not, miss," he continued. "I swear I would not. I did not. I only tried to …"

"He is dead," Victor announced loudly.

I hissed. "Victor, you do not know that. You do not know anything."

"I do," he said simply.

He extricated himself from Lucille's grip, and she let him. Mrs. van Kirk's sobs had turned into wails. Then, he slammed the door shut.

"I apologize for Victor's behavior. I know you would never do such a thing, Williams." Lucille sighed. Then she turned to me and said, "I apologize for my own."

THE NEXT TIME THE DOCTOR ENTERED THE ROOM, HE pronounced Mr. van Kirk dead. I didn't want to believe it, but even I knew the life had long drained out of him. Victor's accusations hung in the air, though we all assured Williams that he would not be forced to leave the manor. He began to cry in earnest. I thought he cried even louder than Mrs. van Kirk did.

February 1886

T HE NOTE ARRIVED THE DAY AFTER MR. VAN KIRK'S DEATH. JANE BROUGHT ME THE FOLDED IVORY PAPER WITH MY NAME written in large, loopy handwriting. The note requested that I accompany the sender to town on the morrow, per Mr. van Kirk's orders prior to his death. The sender apologized for asking something of me so soon, and when I peered closer, I saw Williams's signature at the very bottom.

I passed the note back to Jane. "Do you think this unusual?"

She scanned the note, her head shaking infinitesimally. She returned it to me and said that she'd seen Williams clutching a letter with the hunched red raven in his hand earlier that day.

"Is that so?"

"Yes, Miss Charlotte," she nodded. "But I know nothing of its contents. Most of us have not recovered from the shock of the master's death. Though we do our best to keep the manor, we may not be as sharp."

I placed the note on my desk, thinking to put it out of my mind for the rest of the evening. I couldn't imagine why it was so important to go into town. But in the back of my mind, I remembered Mr. van Kirk requesting the very same thing, groggy as he'd been.

I resolved to wake early on the morrow.

Mr. van Kirk had told me once that Jones was a plain, balding man who prided himself on his ability to afford his wife fashionable clothes and a satisfied belly. He had no children, but if he did, Mr. van Kirk imagined that he'd spoil them as well. I asked him once whether Jones was a greedy man, and he told me Jones was not greedy, but he had no qualms about serving greedy men.

I thought about this description as I walked from the carriage to Jones's office. Williams opened the carriage door for me, helped me climb down, and said nothing about what was to come. I asked for no details, as the letter he clutched in his hand was answer enough.

Once we were inside, Jones's secretary greeted us. She ushered us into his office, which was not overly large, though it was good-sized for a man of business. The desk was cluttered with paperwork. Yet the room afforded just the right amount of fresh air.

"Miss Herring," Jones greeted me. "It is unfortunate

that this meeting takes place under the circumstances. I am very sorry for your loss. Mr. van Kirk was a good man, a very good man."

I nodded and then said, "Frankly, I am not quite sure what circumstances we are under."

"Williams has not yet told you?" Jones asked, incredulous.

My gaze slid to Williams. "No."

"Why, I am taken aback. It falls to me to deliver the news then!"

"I have the letter," Williams informed him. "I am not to give it to Miss Charlotte until after we speak to you."

Jones scratched the side of his head. "Of course. Please, sit down."

Cautiously, I lowered myself onto the nearest chair. Williams stood behind me and tucked the letter into his coat pocket. Jones walked around his desk and seated himself. Immediately, he began rummaging through papers in order to lay out several in front of me.

The papers overlapped one another, and I could only catch glimpses of the words. I knew, though, even as I searched for the heading, that this was Mr. van Kirk's will. How could it not be when he had sent me to Jones?

"Do tell me what is happening," I said.

Jones ran a hand over his face to mask the small smile that was emerging. "I apologize if I seem out of sorts. It is so rare that I get to deliver good news myself in the business I am in, you understand. I, of course, get requests to hand over property or valuable items to descendants all the time, but I was asked to make a change that delighted me for you."

"For me?" I pressed.

He paused, as if for dramatic effect. "For you, Miss Herring. By the request of one Mr. Morton van Kirk, you are to inherit much of the estate."

"Me?" I turned to Williams, but his face was passive.

"Yes, Miss Herring, you. I must admit, I was quite surprised myself when Mr. van Kirk called on me. Even when he was ill, he continued to call on me urgently. But I could not have been happier to oblige him given the circumstances."

I stared hard at Jones's smiling face. "You continue to speak of circumstances, but I am unaware of them. You must not keep me in the dark. I am anxious to know the details of it all."

"Most unfortunate, but that"—Jones said, his smile fading—"is not for me to tell. He insisted upon telling you himself."

"The letter," I murmured.

"The letter," Williams repeated, patting his pocket. "Should you like to read it now, Miss Charlotte?"

My hands shook as I took the letter from Williams. Jones handed me a letter opener, and I slid it under the flap of the envelope in one fluid motion. The seal broke off. I pulled out the writing paper inside, unfolding it slowly.

Dear Charlotte,

If you are reading this, then you must have found yourself in rather peculiar circumstances. I am dead—hopefully, my death was quick and painless. You know I despise lengthy confrontations. Yet, I must leave you with much to ponder.

I have spoken to you of Calcutta on more than one occasion, but I have never had the courage to tell you the whole story. I was young and carefree. I fell in love, Charlotte. I fell in love with a woman named Margaery Herring, whose station was far below my own. You must recognize the last name and forgive me for not telling you all I knew sooner.

But I could not stay in India forever, for I had responsibilities at Ivywood to attend to. I chose to bring her with me. I leased a cottage in town. It was bliss until my family reminded me of my duty—I was promised long ago to Dorothea. I was told she would give me children and a small fortune from her dowry, even after the rumors began circulating about Margaery.

Margaery refused to see me after she learned of Dorothea. She was angry with me. She was angry that I'd brought her onto soil where she could not dig her roots. I did not know she was with child, nor that she would not survive your birth.

How could I, when she would not speak to me? You

*were sent to an orphanage without my knowledge. I
never would have left you there for that long if I'd
known.*

*Dorothea and I married in front of our families, and
I told myself that I had no regrets; it was not true.
Dorothea became with child not long after our marriage.
Victor would be my heir, but I could not celebrate.*

*When I found you, I did not know I would take you in.
I did not know I would put you in an environment
in which a woman would already hate you for what
you were. You have her eyes, you see. Her skin, her
everything. You are too much like her for Dorothea to
not see who you are to me.*

*For some time, I have considered the matter of my
estate, and I cannot justify Victor inheriting Ivywood
Manor. His propensity to live lavishly and his constant
accumulation of debt does not bode well. For those
reasons, I leave you with responsibility of the estate.*

*Trust in Williams, as I have trusted in him, to tell you
what you need to hear. Dorothea is not as cold-hearted
as she seems, so be easy with her. She loves Victor too
much. I apologize for not telling you sooner. I only
wanted you to grow up in a happy home.*

*With love,
Your Father*

When I finished reading the letter, I handed it back to Williams. I could not think, let alone speak. Williams said nothing, but Jones spoke rapidly. He celebrated for me, explaining that this had great implications for my future. He spoke of the estate, investments into other properties, and managing spending. I would be well taken care of. Victor's future, however, looked much gloomier. And it was all thanks to the father I didn't think I knew.

I PEERED AT THE FACE IN THE MIRROR, AND I KNEW I was not white. My eyes weren't sky blue. They weren't hazel or mocha brown. No. They were jungle green, too exotic to be inherited from an ordinary white woman. Was I exotic?

I laid on my bed and lifted the skirts of my apricot silk gown. Slippers, ankles, calves. Was this the color of skin that has been hidden beneath petticoats? How many times did Mrs. van Kirk and Victor tell me it was not? My gaze shifted to my arms, holding the skirts up. Were they the color of arms that spent hours working in the sun? Even Lucille had seen what I had not.

I had no freckles splattered across my face to indicate the sun's role.

I sat up, and I saw the face in the mirror. This wasn't the color one got from walking in the sun with a bonnet to shield one's face. This wasn't the color one got from wearing layers of muslin and silk to cover up arms and legs. I was a shade darker than Victor, and if I glanced at myself quickly, I would never have noticed. This skin was a shade of brown.

I was brown, wasn't I?

But I wasn't hickory brown. I wasn't that deep shade of brown that forces white people to mark me as a foreigner. Did that mean that I wasn't brown?

No, of course not. I had always known that I was brown. My hair might have been straight, but it was black, and my eyes might have been almond-shaped, but they were green. I was exotic, exotic, exotic like tulip trees in the colonies to an Englishman who couldn't resist a beautiful woman. He said so himself.

I had held the proof in my hands. The words were written on paper, so new that I knew they must have been written not long after he'd taken ill. He'd wanted me to know, but he wasn't ready to tell me.

And I knew this too.

I was never exotic, no. I was human. I was white. I was brown. I could be both; I was both. Maybe that's what he feared—that I was too much of everything. Too many memories of a woman he loved, a woman he betrayed, and a son he'd ruined.

He took me in and deliberately let me keep my mother's name, but what for? Because he loved me as a Herring, but never as a van Kirk. Did he love me with the blood of another race running through my veins? Or did he love me despite it? I didn't know. Would I ever?

"Where are you from, Williams?" I asked.

I sat in front of my dresser with my hands folded in my lap. Jane stood behind me, her fingers separating strands of my hair into three sections. She began weaving, one section overlapping another until she reached the very ends of my hair. Williams stood beside her, and his eyes met my own in the mirror.

"I was raised at Ivywood Manor, Miss Charlotte," he replied. "My mother was a chambermaid, and the master's father was kind enough to let me stay on."

"Ivywood is home to you," I said.

Williams contemplated the statement. "The only home I have known is one with the van Kirks. They have treated my family very well over the years, and I have served them as they saw fit."

I stared down at my fingers, fiddling and testing the softness of them. They weren't hardened by manual labor or worn by life in a factory. They wouldn't feel the way they did now if Mr. van Kirk had not taken me in. How could he not have taken me in if I was his daughter?

"You knew all this time," I breathed. "Why did no one tell me?"

I raised my eyes, and I saw Jane staring particularly hard at the brush on my dresser. I knew then that she knew as well. Whether she'd known from the start, I couldn't be sure, and I didn't care to ask.

"Does everyone know?" I asked instead.

"You must understand, Miss Charlotte. I could not

tell you. We did not speak of it, or her, after she refused to see your father," Williams explained.

Jane nodded.

I closed my eyes. "Margaery. Her name was Margaery, and she was my mother."

"Oh! Do not think I did not care for your mother, Miss Charlotte," Williams said firmly. "I cared for her greatly. How could we not, with the master being so taken with her? She had such a kind heart."

A thought occurred to me, and I opened my eyes. "Has Victor known this whole time? Lucille? Everyone?"

Williams replied, "The master did not see fit to inform Victor of your heritage, nor did the lady of the manor. She did not wish to cast a pall over his rights as heir to the van Kirks, so to speak. He will, however, have met with Jones this afternoon, and his suspicions will be confirmed."

"I do not think his new bride knows everything," Jane added. "He has only given her hints of what he suspects."

"He has squandered much of her fortune," Williams admitted grudgingly. "Repaying his debts. He has taken to gambling now, but without the estate, he has no source of income. He will not take the news lightly."

I grimaced. "And what is Lucille's part in this?"

"If I may, Miss Charlotte," Jane said quietly, "I believe she knows that you are more than a child adopted at random, though I doubt Victor has shared everything with her. She does not wish for him to ruin the family, and she cares for you so.”

I stared at my own face in the mirror hard. I was angry, so angry that I'd been denied the knowledge of my birth for so long. I hadn't understood why Mrs. van Kirk despised my presence or Victor treated me with contempt. I hadn't known if Mr. van Kirk truly favored me or pitied me. All those times I'd asked him for information, he had denied me. But now it made no matter.

Jane's eyes were cast downward, ashamed at having kept the secret from me. Williams, on the other hand, didn't flinch. He was as proud as ever, stubborn in the idea that he had done his duty to the van Kirks by keeping his silence. And I had no one else to turn to besides them. Why else did they let me wander the halls or enter their quarters with no regard for propriety?

“We wanted the best for you,” Williams said. “We tried to shield you from her anger.”

And I believed him.

“What now? Victor has practically trussed you up for Mr. van Kirk's death, Williams! It is on the rest of our word that you remain employed. And now he grows angry at Lucille. We must stop him.”

“Miss Charlotte, it is not my place—”

“Hang your place, Williams!” I insisted. “Your place is with me. If anyone runs Ivywood to the ground, it will be Victor. This, at least, I have always known.”

After Williams and I came back from Jones's office, Victor said nothing. He didn't pause to disparage me for the blood running through my veins or refute the claims of my heritage or shout that the contents of the will were an outrage. Instead, he flapped from one room to the next, as if he were a bird that had flown into the manor but couldn't find its way out.

He remained like that for two days. He spoke to no one except Lucille and the servants. The invitations from the gentlemen and ladies of society to Victor and Lucille as newlyweds stopped altogether. Instead, I received letters addressed to me in the hope that I'd settle business matters, and I was made aware in a way that I never had been before of the extent of Victor's debts.

Lucille's dowry had rid Victor of almost all his troubles initially, but his continued spending could not be maintained. There were more orders for furniture and paintings from Venice. There were payments covering his high society friends' expenses, most likely to display his own wealth. There were tabs that had yet to be closed at gentlemen's clubs both in Europe and in town. His new gambling habit since he'd been wed had greatly diminished Lucille's coffers. But when I tried to speak to Victor of his financial straits, he stomped into the library and slammed the door shut behind him.

Though it didn't belong to him, Victor made a gilded cage out of that room. Behind the bars, he was safe from my prying eyes. The sole comfort I took was in the idea that others were not burdened by his presence.

I resolved to speak to Lucille, but I didn't wish to do so in Mrs. van Kirk's presence.

Mrs. van Kirk was acting as if nothing had changed. She ordered the servants to clean this or that table, requested chicken fricassee from Molly, and fawned over Lucille. I found her behavior so normal that I asked her whether she had anything to say on the subject.

She sniffed and said, "I knew it would be this way since he found you."

"Did you know my mo—"

"She was before me," Mrs. van Kirk continued. "Must we speak of her?"

I pursed my lips. "You know that Victor's spending is—"

"I have no control over him," she snapped. "He is aware of his standing in this family. You must speak to him."

Later that night, I asked Jane to slip a letter to Lucille. It detailed everything I knew about Victor's debts. Then it asked that she meet with me whenever it suited her best.

I didn't expect such a prompt reply.

Lucille knocked on my bedroom door mere minutes after receiving my note. Her hair was neat, but her face was distraught. When she spoke, her normally high, melodic voice sounded frantic and her words jumbled.

"I did not know the extent of it," she whispered. "The match appeared favorable from the outset, and I noted his spending in Venice, but I cannot speak to him of this, Charlotte. It would only anger him further. He mutters things under his breath—unspeakable words. He is my husband, but I do not know how to act around him."

"What sort of unspeakable words?" I asked.

She averted her gaze. "He mumbles them. I do not…he calls you a—a half-caste. He's very angry with you. He thought he was inheriting the estate, Charlotte."

"I cannot help where I come from," I reminded her.

"Oh, Charlotte! I did not mean it that way at all! I cannot tell him to curb his spending. If I do, I worry that he'll do something drastic."

I could think of nothing else to do at the moment, so I told Lucille that I would speak to her again about the matter if I managed to come up with a solution.

March 1886

For some time, I kept a close eye on Victor. I folded letters and smashed them between the pages of journals and books. I didn't address them to anyone, and I wrote with my left hand so that the script became rather illegible because Lucille had told me Victor was suspicious of everyone. I left them everywhere—slipped them onto tea trays, pushed them under doorways, and asked Jane to stuff them into dress pockets.

I received my answers in a similar manner. Jane laid her responses on my writing desk. Molly sent warm milk up to my bedroom without my asking for it. Williams left them with groomsmen in the stables and suggested it was a lovely day to go riding.

There was nothing Victor did that I didn't know about. He was becoming increasingly erratic as we watched him. He was no longer receiving letters from his so-called friends, and he was no longer welcomed at the gentlemen's club. I'd paid off his debts, but his credit was not to be trusted. Forced to spend his time at Ivywood, he snapped at servants for looking in his direction and scolded Lucille for the time she spent eating or talking. Nothing could appease him, and that was what I was afraid of most.

Two letters arrived that day. One peeked out from under my pillow, and the other sat on my writing desk. The first was from Lucille, and it was exceedingly short in length. The other was from Jack.

I asked Jane to sit by my side as I opened the groundskeeper's letter. It read:

Last night, I heard voices arguing near the cottage. I stepped outside to tell them off, thinking it was some strangers who had snuck onto the property, but it was not. It was the young master, Miss Charlotte.

I saw his profile, and the rest of him was in shadow. He was talking to someone. I could not see the other person's face. They were arguing, though I do not know what about. He was saying it was 'his business,' not the other's. The missus came out to look for me, and she spooked them quiet.

I had no choice but to return home. I am writing this now before the missus comes to tell me to get back to bed. She thinks it must be his bride, but she says it has nothing to do with us. I do not know what it means, but I do not want to forget anything.

My hands were steady as I folded the note up and handed it to Jane. She read it quietly and shook her head. She kept muttering that it was dangerous what we were doing. I told her that she shouldn't worry, but when she handed me Lucille's note, I found that my hands began to shake.

The note contained a few short lines:

Charlotte, Victor and I got into a tiff last night. He suspects I am going against him somehow. I denied it, of course. But he is very angry with me. Do not concern yourself over me by visiting. It will only make him angrier. I am not afraid.

I woke with a start in the early morning hours; it was the third time I'd roused to no sound in the manor other than my rapid pulse beating. I turned my head to rest the left side of my face on the pillow and lay there. Then, I turned my head the opposite way, squeezing my eyes shut, unable to bring myself to sleep. *I am not afraid*, Lucille had said. Yet I remembered Jack's letter, and I was afraid for her.

Victor was unpredictable. His anger was building like the flaky remnants of cigars piling up in an ashtray he'd yet to discard. All he wanted was for someone to provoke him—someone to toss the residue at.

I lay there for another minute before I rose from bed, resolving to check on Lucille. I left my room, crept down the hall with my hand running along the wall, and paused outside of Lucille's door. I knocked softly, fearing I would cause a stir. Predictably, she didn't respond.

Tentatively, I turned the doorknob and pushed lightly. There was a small gap, from which I could see the outline of Lucille's body in the dark. She lay still, and I whispered her name several times, but she gave no indication of having heard me.

I pushed the door open farther so that I could enter the room and closed it behind me. I called out to her once more. Then I came closer and noticed something odd: she was not under the bedsheets. Why would she be on top of them?

Every step forward took effort. My legs shook, unwilling to take me on a straight path to her. Only when I was right beside her could I see her more clearly, and my hands shuddered as I reached out to touch her face.

Her skin was pale, and harsh purple marks stood out on her neck. Her blue eyes, which had once been so wide and innocent, were partially open, as if someone had attempted to shutter them from the sight of herself. Creases lined her forehead, illustrating the confusion that had taken place during the struggle.

My eyes began to fill, and I shoved the despair down. Lucille was dead. Someone had murdered her, and though I dreaded the answer, I knew who.

Was he to blame? Or was this my burden to bear?

I backed away from her body and out of the room. Then I headed down the stairs to the servants' quarters. I woke Williams first, and he in turn woke the rest of the servants. They began to swarm in and out of the rooms, calling for one another to fetch this or that—bedsheets, doctors, and police.

In the midst of it all, I watched Victor move to the foot of Lucille's bed. His face was turned toward the open window, half in shadow as the sun rose in the sky. He acted as if he didn't hear me approach or the noise outside the door or the chaos that had brought him here in the first place.

THE FAMILY DOCTOR CAME TO EXAMINE THE BODY, speaking to Victor in soft tones about the tragedy that was such a young girl's death. He couldn't imagine why someone would kill her. No one else besides Victor and myself had ventured into the room where her body lay, and no one wished to.

"She appears to have suffered trauma to the neck," the doctor told Victor in a hushed voice. "But I cannot say the cause of death yet."

Victor stood at the foot of the bed with his hands clasped together behind his back and simply nodded.

He refused to take his gaze away from the doctor who stood adjacent to him. The doctor had covered Lucille's body with a bedsheet, but the mere outline was disturbing to the eye.

I positioned myself on the opposite side of the doctor, near Lucille's side. My fingers were mere inches away from Lucille's, but I was numb to the coldness emanating from her hand. I couldn't bear to leave her quite yet.

She'd warned me last night, and I'd done nothing.

"Shall we—" the doctor began.

I couldn't help but insert myself into the conversation. "What do you mean by trauma to the neck? She has been strangled, can you not see?"

"Charlotte, he has given his diagnosis," Victor said dully. "There is no need to trouble him further."

Victor turned away from the bed and walked to the door. He gestured to the exit, wanting both the doctor and myself to follow him. The doctor did as he was asked, continuing to speak in hushed tones. I, on the other hand, refused to leave.

The knock came soon after. The doorknob turned, and the soft patter of footsteps neared. Someone gently touched my shoulder. I turned.

There were deep lines on Jane's forehead where her eyebrows were drawn together. The look was one of confusion, which hadn't disappeared since I'd told her what had happened. But she didn't remove her hand.

I could see Williams at the door, engaged in a

heated argument with Victor. Victor kept pointing toward Lucille's body. He was glaring, and I knew that Williams was most certainly speaking out of turn to grant me these few moments alone.

"He will be in more trouble," Jane muttered. "At least he no longer has the authority to replace him."

"This is not right."

"No, Miss Charlotte," Jane agreed. "It is not."

I watched Victor throw his hands up in the air. "He wants me to leave her side?"

Jane nodded. "The doctor wants to examine her body again, but he says he cannot do so with you by her side. Williams is trying to give you some time."

"It is no use," I said, leaving Lucille. "Has someone contacted Lucille's family?"

Williams stepped aside, grimacing. "I have sent for the Kings. The doctor would like the room, though I am loath to give it to him. Perhaps you should rest, Miss Charlotte. If you require anything, I will send for it immediately."

I patted Williams on the arm. "That is not necessary, Williams. I am rested, only very distressed. He has killed her, Williams."

Williams eyes were downcast. "He has, miss."

THE KINGS WERE TRAVELING WHEN THEY RECEIVED the news of their only daughter's death, and they arrived at Ivywood Manor in utter despair. They approached the raven statues, stood under their glare, and said that the manor must have been cursed all along. I knew better. The ravens were only an omen, the squawks a warning, and the feeding yet to come.

They hired a private detective, who was said to be a discreet man, to investigate Lucille's death. Not long after arriving, he claimed he would be following various leads. He said the inhabitants of the manor had given them to him, but I knew he'd gotten them from Victor. Lucille had been murdered, and I couldn't count on the detective for justice.

Victor, I'd been told, had led the detective down into the servants' quarters the night he arrived. He'd urged the detective to question every person who'd ever come into contact with Lucille. He seemed determined to resurrect every piece of information about the servants' pasts that he could find. They spent twice the amount of time questioning Williams as anyone else.

The Kings left after a week, but the detective stayed. I was surprised that he didn't knock on my door, too.

April 1886

At half past one, I entered the library in search of solace after Lucille's death. The door creaked open, revealing an unlit fire and the glow of the moon shining through the window. I navigated the room in nothing but my nightgown with a dim candle to guide me.

The friction of my feet against the rug created a slow shuffling sound. My gown rustled against the shelves as I edged around the room. I let my fingers rise and fall, tracing the shapes of book covers.

Intermittently, I paused. Flashes of Lucille, her body on top of those sheets, popped into my head. She'd been so pale and cold. Those marks on her neck were made by a man who was desperate for control. Yet how could he have any when I was responsible for the manor?

I was so furious that my hands began to shake.

Thinking it best to sit down, I went to Mr. van Kirk's desk and tried to push the thoughts aside. It was difficult, as his desk looked not at all like it had been before. It was too uncluttered; there were no papers scattered over its surface, nor were there books precariously balancing atop one another.

I opened a drawer and was saddened to discover nothing but ordinary pens and papers that shifted and rattled as I closed it again. I don't know what I thought I'd find. I hoped to incriminate Victor in the crime he'd committed, but it was a futile effort.

I pushed away from the chair and walked toward the settee. There was a book lying on the table, half of it hanging over the edge. It was as if the reader had carelessly tossed it there, and I was certain it must've been Victor.

I picked it up, running my finger over its spine, and then I flipped it over to examine the cover.

It was one of Mr. van Kirk's travel diaries. I recognized his handwriting on the cover, the unnecessary space left between each letter in "India." I flipped through the pages, and I found that the volume contained all his entries from his stay there. I felt sure that this diary was the same one he'd said was more poetic than any other book I'd read.

It was not in my nature to be nervous, but I was. I turned to a random page and ran my fingers over the indents made there by the press of pen against paper. Then, I began reading.

19 October 1850

Mr. Albertson, the collector, hosted a party to welcome Henry's friends from London yesterday. I believe he invited every prominent, wealthy Englishman and Indian he'd ever met! Henry insisted that I accompany him, but I spent most of the time conversing with Mr. Albertson about trade and people I needed to know to get ahead in this country.

Every time we crossed paths with someone, Mr. Albertson insisted upon introducing me. I'd met most everyone already, and I told him so. He simply responded that I hadn't met the Herring family because they didn't often attend these events. It was true that it would be to my advantage to know them, and I was curious. I'd heard a great deal about their wealth, if not their station.

I convinced Mr. Albertson to wait a little before approaching them, and when we did, Mr. Albertson had twice the enthusiasm as usual. He introduced us to one another and asked the Herrings how they were enjoying the party so far. Mr. Herring responded that everything was splendid, and it was confirmed as soon as he spoke that he was a very important man to the community.

Mr. Herring was tall and slightly rounded with graying hair and blue eyes. He spoke with a deep, authoritative tone that I was hard-pressed to ignore.

But what took me aback was his wife. Her name was Mahuri, and she was a beautiful Indian woman with these bright green eyes. When I met her gaze, I saw pride in it rather than the demure quality that lingered in an English woman's pupils.

His daughter, Margaery, was equally, if not more, startling. The very first thing I noticed was that she had her mother's eyes. She carried herself more confidently, gracefully, than any other woman I'd met so far. And she was tall, almost as tall as her father. I could scarcely believe I was seeing her.

After more pleasantries, the males and females separated. I spent the rest of the party trying to hold Mr. Herring's attention, chatting with him about polo and policies. All the while, my gaze wandered toward the women mingling across the way.

I knew that if her father took a liking to me, I was more likely to be in his daughter's presence, and I was determined to do so, if nothing more.

I don't know how long I stared at that entry, but by the time I closed the book and looked around, I felt the strain on my eyes. This was the day that my parents had met, that my father became enchanted with my mother before she even opened her mouth. I knew that he was going to love her, and I wondered how that love could have caused so much death.

I spent the next night searching for the rest of Mr. van Kirk's travel diaries. It seemed that Victor had only managed to find the India one, but I located some from Europe among the French books I'd studied. I almost wondered if Mr. van Kirk had left them there before he died so that I could find them. Their spines creaked and cracked when I opened them, and I knew they had not been touched.

After browsing the Europe volumes, I settled into the settee with the book about India. Then, I began reading my mother and father's story.

After the first time my father set eyes on my mother, he took every opportunity to be by her side. Every word that left her mouth was charming. He praised her intelligence and her witty remarks and compared her to his duller companions throughout his time in India.

He wrote of how he felt standing beside her before statues of Hanuman, mosques, and stupas alike. My mother was always dressed in clothes the color of tikka powders: the red of new blood shed, the green of well-watered bushes, and the blue of sapphires set in stones. And I saw her beauty through my father's eyes when he was younger and his countenance brighter.

He was in love because she was new and exotic to him. There was a difference in the way he penned her name, almost as if the feeling was too overwhelming to keep his hand steady. The "M" in her name was always larger, more slanted than any other, while the rest was scribbled in a rush to get his thoughts on the page. She was untouchable.

But nothing cemented my father's love for her more than the entry in which he described the day he asked my mother to come to England.

7 January 1853

I met Margaery today before the Raj Bhavan, the government house with wrought iron gates and statues of massive lions surrounded by acres of formal gardens. I felt the shadow of the three-storied building bearing down on me as I waited for her. She came to me, rounding curved corridors and moving between detached wings, and I thought how well I'd come to know the sound of bangles clanging against one another, the glint of her earrings, and the draping of saffron-colored cloth over her body.

I greeted her as I always did, and we strolled in the gardens. We conversed about the weather, the sheer magnificence of the Raj Bhavan, and the green in her eyes. I believe she knew what I was about to ask her before I knew it myself. She was intelligent; she'd proven that many a time.

I told her I needed to return home soon, that I was wanted. She expressed that she would be saddened to see me go. We were about to part! How could I let her go? I asked her rather unceremoniously if she'd come with me.

I didn't think about what I was asking of her. She would not be welcomed. I knew my father and mother too well to expect anything different. But I could provide for her now, and I couldn't bear to part with her.

I practically shouted it at her! I calmed myself enough to tell her she need not reply right away, and she didn't. It is agony, but I must wait until tomorrow to hear from her. How can she say no?

I read that entry twice, closing my eyes and trying to imagine what the weight of three stories felt like, how deeply a person had to feel to understand what my father was feeling when he'd written it. He had told me of the Raj Bhavan before, had described every important person who'd walked in and out of its doors. But I had never known what the site truly meant to him until I read the entry where she said yes.

He brought her here, not to Ivywood, but to a leased cottage—another story he'd neglected to tell me fully. She lived there for two years before she became pregnant with me, but she didn't tell him. I only know the day I was born because he wrote of it later with anger in the form of jabs so sharp they left holes in the paper.

Her servants kept the secret of me growing inside her, while he spoke of his time with the Mrs. van Kirk

I'd come to know. When my mother found out, she was furious. I know this because he wrote of her voice echoing against the walls and reverberating in his ears. That was before she refused to see him.

He raged and seethed at her doorway, but the servants were as loyal to her as they were to him. He couldn't be angry with anyone who dedicated themselves so fully to the woman he loved. She was a prize that he'd lost but hoped to regain.

Yet before he knew it, my mother was lost forever.

Everything in the travel diaries felt abrupt, too much or too little. I wanted to know more about her, less about the politics of everyday life. I wanted to see her, not only hear about the cultural aspects that my father found so fascinating. I wanted to hear her, not my father. I hardly knew how to grieve for my mother when all his words spoke of her foreignness, let alone read of my father's wedding to a suitable English woman.

I forced myself to finish reading the diaries, to learn at the same time as he learned of my existence and my mother's death, and only when I knew everything of importance did I close the volume.

I spent the earlier part of the morning taking a walk along the grounds, thinking of my mother and father. I wondered what she would've said if she could tell her story. Did she love my father as much as he loved her? I dwelled on all the things my father hadn't bothered to tell me. Then, I recalled every snide comment made about my skin, and how he'd tried and failed to protect me.

To take my mind off the travel diaries, I wandered near the cottages to check on Jack. He rambled about his upcoming plans to tidy up the inside of his home at first but became awkward when I turned the conversation toward the note he'd written about Lucille and Victor's fight. I asked whether he knew anything else that could be of use, but he said that he didn't.

"Are you certain you cannot remember anything else from that night?"

"Only what I told you, miss. That's all."

"I suppose I should not have expected more," I said with a sigh. "You look concerned."

Jack kept looking back to the cottage. "I only worry, you see, miss, about you investigating the murder yourself. The situation seems dangerous…considering. And what are *we* to do if you get yourself into trouble?"

"I will not, Jack."

"Helen says I am not doing right. I don't know if am or if you are. I don't know much of anything anymore. None of us do."

"That's understandable."

He intoned, "You should take care."

On top of all that I'd learned, I didn't want to put

too much thought into his warnings, so I thanked him and moved on.

The door to the library was ajar, and I heard rustling within. I rapped lightly on the door with my knuckles before pushing it open and entering. Victor stood beside a bookcase on the left, his fingers frozen over the spine of a book tilted just so to see the title on the cover. Upon seeing me, he let the book hang by his side as his eyes swept over me.

"Are you in search of something, Charlotte?" he asked.

"I only thought I heard someone in here, and I grew most curious."

Victor carefully placed the book back on a shelf. He walked toward the table before the settee in the middle of the library. There was a pile of ledgers that hadn't been there the night before. He moved to stand in front of them in an attempt to block my sight.

"That is the difficulty with women," he said, snarling. "Curiosity."

"You do not approve of a curious mind?" I asked.

"I do not approve of a woman sticking her nose where it does not belong," he clarified. "Especially in my affairs. You understand, do you not?"

"I have read many a book that touted the same philosophy," I admitted. "But your affairs are as much as mine now."

"I am sure you can find another book that will tell

you otherwise. Our father gave you free rein of his book collection, did he not?"

The words were tinged with bitterness, and Victor turned his back to me. He knew I'd get riled up if he taunted me enough. He was only waiting for it to happen. I refused to take the bait.

Victor began shutting all the ledgers before I could get closer. The sound was akin to someone dropping a heavy, dust-riddled tome from a considerable height. I flinched as I watched his fingers wrap around and press into every spine much harder than he needed to.

"I am certain you were never banned from the library," I told Victor. "Our father welcomed most anyone in."

"Yes," he muttered, turning back around. "Anyone. It is a…difficult time right now, so let us not speak of this."

I scoffed. "I feel the loss of him and Lucille, but I am sure not as hard as you do, Victor."

Victor smoothed his hand over his suit and then picked up a book from a nearby shelf. He shoved the book into my hands. I glanced down at it. I asked him whether he had an interest in traveling to India, and he laughed.

"It is you that has an interest in them," he stated.

"Perhaps I have already taken an interest in them."

He sniggered. "If that is the case, then you know for certain that you are a half-caste. You will never be anything more. You cannot be."

Without hesitation, he piled the ledgers into his arm and returned them to the top of Mr. van Kirk's desk.

He walked around to sit in the seat that I had never thought of as his. Then he lifted an arm to gesture to the rest of the library, as if saying, *It's all yours.*

"I am already more, Victor."

I made my way to the door. My hands shook as I clumsily attempted to grasp the doorknob. Once I had it, I flung the door open and left.

I WAS INCENSED FOLLOWING MY ENCOUNTER WITH Victor. He was a starving vulture, barring strangers' entrance into the manor and instilling fear through the brown flecks in his eyes. His wings might have been clipped and tucked in, but they'd grown wild. I recognized it in the way his puce lips stretched into a triumphant smile and his arms spread wide, as if claiming ownership of his prize.

Mrs. van Kirk paid no attention to his gaze, to any of us other than the detective. She could not believe that Lucille had died and resolved to rely only on the detective's final account of the matter, rather than the gossip that it was her son's doing.

At the Kings' request, the detective came and went from the manor. He stayed in one of the cottages because he was still in the process of gathering evidence, though he gave no indication of whom it was against.

Williams, on the other hand, was more observant than ever. He saw how Victor looked at me, steered me away from him in the halls, and warned me when he intended to enter a room. But the servants could only protect me for so long.

THE FLECKS IN VICTOR'S EYES WERE NOT BROWN OR blue or gray; they were black. They were the complete absence of light as he entered my room. His feet were light, stealthy as they maneuvered around my furniture to reach me in bed. I laid there, my face riddled with confusion, and waited.

I thought of the debt he owed to Mr. van Kirk—a copious sum he'd spent in Europe and at home. I recalled the despair on his face after several failed attempts to speak to Mr. van Kirk of his plan to obtain more money. Most of all, I remembered the fateful night I was introduced to his scapegoat: Lucille King.

She'd told me how he'd wined, dined, and practically spit on the shoes of her father in order to be worthy of asking for her hand in marriage. I had only seen Victor lower himself for causes he deemed beneficial to him. He was a van Kirk, set to inherit a large estate before he'd lost everything.

Mr. van Kirk had known. How many times had he begun to tell me of Victor's plight before we were interrupted? How many times had Victor shown himself to be a willful child under the shadow of his mother's protection?

Mr. van Kirk had died, but not before Victor wed Lucille and declared in God's abode an undying love he didn't feel. Lucille knew what their marriage was, though she might not have known the extent of it. And she'd cared for me in a way that she'd never cared for Victor.

He despised it—me. I was not pure, not white. I was the product of an affair between our father and my mother. I was not worthy of Mr. van Kirk's attentions. And I was in the way of his inheritance.

In one fluid movement, Victor climbed atop my bed and straddled me. He was wearing gloves that flashed white in the moonlight. The marks left by his fingers on Lucille's neck would not be prevented from being left on my own by a thin veil of material. He yanked the pillow from beneath my head, and I jerked away.

His clumsy hands reached for me to cover my face with the pillow.

Instinctively, I tried to stop him. I said his name, though the sound was muffled. I asked him what he was doing. I begged him, told him this was not necessary. It didn't have to end like this.

Victor's voice was hoarse when he spoke, barely above a whisper. "I have to. You have ruined it. You are ruining everything."

I struggled beneath the weight of him.

"NO!" Victor hissed. "Stop. Just. Let. Me."

I shook my head violently.

"You know what you've done!" Victor's face screwed up. "You took everything from me! You even tried to take Lucille, did you not?!"

His words gave me pause. *Lucille.*

He was shouting. "My mother cannot know. No one can know. And you know what I have done to her! How can I let you go on?"

I began to thrash, and Victor's hold on the pillow faltered for a second. I thrust my knee up into his abdomen. He groaned, doubling over and clutching his side. I attempted to shove him off the bed, but his legs hadn't moved from their place, and my actions only angered him further.

Tossing the pillow aside, he pinned me with his hands around my throat.

"No," I croaked.

His fingers tightened, and a bead of sweat dripped down his brow. It landed on my cheek. Then it slid down, as if it were my tear, as if the murder of Lucille was his grievance filed against me.

"No," I tried to say again.

But his smile was cruel. The stiff bend to the left side of his lips and the twitch in his jaw were pronounced. He was sweating profusely now from the effort of holding my throat while trying to avoid my flailing limbs—so much so that it seemed he would drown me before I could suffocate.

He kept telling me to stop fighting, but I refused.

No, I wanted to tell him. *I won't die like this. Not at your hands.*

I stretched my fingers so that I could touch his throat. There, I gripped, digging my nails into his skin, and held until his face began to turn blue. He swore, and I stumbled out the door and down the stairs.

Outside, the sky raged against Ivywood Manor, while the moonlight cast a long shadow upon my face. Stormy gray clouds let loose sheets of rain instead of droplets. Too many to count raced down the panes, pushing and shoving each other until I couldn't tell one from the next.

There was no lightning to strike Victor down for the deeds he'd committed, nor for the deed he'd tried to commit. But there was thunder—loud, rolling, rumbling to shake the manor to its very core. I intended to run as far away from Victor as my feet could take me.

Mrs. van Kirk, Williams, and Jane gathered to watch the spectacle I created: yelling, running, and slamming my fist against the doors. Mrs. van Kirk said I was not mentally stable, claiming there was a murderer in the house. Williams and Jane didn't contradict her, but they huddled against each other. They'd heard my shriek, a sound so loud that it scared the ravens from the very perches they'd been built upon.

Victor hadn't dared to follow once I'd woken everyone. I knew that if I let him, he'd clothe me in darkness to keep me warm, as if I were an affronted lover and he only aimed to please me. But I refused to keep silent.

Williams stopped me at the gate of the manor. He'd sent Jane to get the detective from the cottages while he held Victor. I stood there, listening to the squishing sounds of boots in mud and the flap of wings in the distance. I wanted to turn my head, search for another cause for the frenzy. But if I did, would they think I'd try to run?

I had nowhere to go.

Someone shouted, and I gathered the courage to look. The inhabitants of the manor were lining up. One by one, the servants, the ladies, and the gentleman alike neared the gate, and I smelled fear in the staunch, sour odor of sweat.

Victor stood defiantly on the arm of Williams. Sweat intermingled with his own blood on his neck, and mud on his feet caked to his skin like a second layer. He stood upright, but he was small, and he stared at me as if I were a ghost. Beads of water dripped from his hair down his forehead.

"A dream," Victor murmured. Then louder, "I cannot possibly imagine why we are being held out here in this weather."

Then I began to laugh.

The sound wasn't the deep, true sound that comes from one's belly, nor was it the sound of a lady tittering at a piece of gossip. My laugh began from my throat, made me choke on the ridiculousness of it and my body shake from the shoulders down until I was leaning over. If I straightened, they would have known that the laughter did not reach my eyes.

It was so hollow, that sound, that it echoed, resounded against nothing.

"A dream—"

I couldn't continue.

I couldn't fathom the notion that all of this—the blood, Williams, me—were images that anyone would want to dream about. I was nothing but bruised skin, as if someone had tried to press me into wine, but not long enough to age me.

If anything, Victor should've been used to the hideousness he'd created. He must have seen much worse when he held the body of his wife and lover in his hands and choked her till she gasped, struggled, kicked for breath. But he cared for no one but himself.

"It's not a dream," I said to someone, but I didn't know who.

It was a nightmare. There was darkness. Maybe it was him. Or maybe it was me. But he should've been afraid.

In the wee hours of morning, I sat in the servants' quarters across from the detective, and for the first time I really looked at him. He was tall, with bushy eyebrows and untrimmed facial hair. His beard was long enough that I wondered if he'd ever accidentally dipped it in a teacup. I wasn't sure why the detective was conducting my interview in the kitchen, but he said it was the most convenient, for he'd have to talk to everyone within the household before reporting back to the Kings.

Victor, he added, was awfully calm. He was sitting in the informal drawing room with small drops of blood dripping down his neck, staining his dress shirt. When asked whether he'd placed hands on me, he'd only laughed.

The detective pulled out pen and paper, scribbled something down, and then said, "Can you tell me what happened, Miss Herring?"

I stared blankly at him before repeating, "What happened?"

"Yes, miss," he said, raising an eyebrow so high that it seemed it would touch his hairline. "I mean to establish the intent. It is clear that you are both injured, but he seems the less sane."

"He tried to strangle me, detective," I said flatly. "He intended to kill me."

"I can see that, miss. Your butler, Williams, has contacted medical professionals to deal with him. But in the meantime, I would like to get this settled. He has misled me to believe that you might have had a hand in the deaths that have taken place here."

I shook my head slowly. "It is not true."

"Shall we start from the beginning?" he suggested. "How did you come to live in this household?"

The question was one I'd asked myself many times before I learned of my true parentage. I had never understood why Mr. van Kirk chose me, but Nancy had taught all of the orphans not to question when strangers inquired after us. If we were fortunate enough to be considered for adoption, there were no questions of importance to ask. We were blessed to be given a home, and Nancy was blessed to have one less mouth to feed.

I was certain that the detective didn't care for my musings, so I said, "I was adopted."

He repressed a sigh. He tapped the pen against his thigh. "At what age would you say that was?"

"Nine," I replied. "What has this to do with—"

He interrupted me. "What do you know of Mr. van Kirk's death, Miss Herring?"

"The doctors ruled it inconclusive," I said, frustrated. "He had a high fever for days, and his health deteriorated quickly. That is all we were told."

"Is that so?" He made a *hmmm* sound. "Have you suspected foul play in that as well?"

"Yes."

"I have obtained information that he was already ill, but by an overdose of laudanum, his death was sped up, it seems. And what do you know of the death of a Miss Lucille van Kirk?"

I glowered at the floor, but my voice was steady. "She was strangled."

The detective's face took on some sympathy. His eyebrows were lower and his jaw softer, so that his beard shifted with him. "I am sorry if this is difficult for you, but can you identify the murderer?"

"Victor," I said slowly. "Victor van Kirk."

He nodded, writing down the name. "And you were born to Morton van Kirk and recently designated as his heir in his will?"

"Yes."

He bobbed his head, his gaze focused on my face. Whatever appeared there, I wasn't sure. But he must've been satisfied, since he moved on.

"Mrs. van Kirk has admitted to knowing you would be named heir since Mr. van Kirk took ill," he continued.

"She has?"

He ignored my question. "It's been said that Victor van Kirk has been behaving erratically since he returned home from abroad."

I tilted my head to the side. "Not at first, but I suppose you could say that…"

"What can you tell me about it?" he asked, leaning back so that his chair rocked on its hind legs.

From his posture, I assumed that the questions were not likely to end anytime soon. So I straightened my back and held onto the seat of the chair with both hands. And I continued to answer.

The men cloaked in black came in a carriage with metal bars. They held shackles and chains to use, if deemed necessary, to restrain Victor. They ran a private insane asylum, which Williams had contacted to keep the series of scandalous events as quiet as possible. Mrs.

van Kirk was the first to greet them; her face was stone, but her hands shook tremendously.

"It cannot be …" she muttered.

Victor was escorted out of his room by the detective and Williams. He put up no struggle and only chuckled when someone addressed him. I walked behind him with Jane by my side. She pressed my hands between hers as we watched him be handed off to the doctors.

They placed him into the carriage behind lock and key. The silver glinted as the sun rose above the horizon, flamingo pink flashes into the blackness. One of the doctors parted from the group with papers in hand and approached Mrs. van Kirk.

"Where will they take him?" I asked.

Williams answered with a grimace. "He will live more comfortably than he deserves, Miss Charlotte. The asylum has a parlor, a kitchen, long entries, and many rooms. It looks to be a heavily guarded estate from afar."

I rubbed the sides of my neck but stopped when I felt Mrs. van Kirk's gaze on me. Her eyes were filled with horror as she took in the colors blooming in the sky. She numbly gestured to me.

"Are you the head of the household?" the doctor asked.

"I— Yes, I suppose I am."

He handed me the papers to sign, consenting to Victor's move to the asylum. I signed and handed them to him. He thanked me before returning to the carriage.

Mrs. van Kirk appeared by my side, murmuring. "How could this have happened?"

"I suppose it is not as unlikely as I once thought it to be."

In response, Mrs. van Kirk fanned herself with her hand and walked into the manor before she could witness Victor being taken away. I stayed and watched the carriage roll until I couldn't see its wheels anymore. Once it was gone, I made my way inside, shivering.

I ENTERED THE KITCHEN AND SAT IN THE CHAIR THE detective had questioned me in. I couldn't sit still, my eyes darting from the oven to the ingredients lining the shelves. Williams, Jane, Molly, and Jack surrounded me. The manor was eerily quiet. Mrs. van Kirk hadn't left her room since Victor was taken away.

When I looked around, I saw sunken eyes and drooping mouths. Molly kept offering to make everyone a cup of tea, but only Jack accepted. Helen scolded him from her corner of the room but offered no other resistance.

Molly bustled around, tidying the kitchen as she waited to hear the kettle whistle.

"Miss Charlotte, are you all right?" Jane asked.

"I am," I replied, patting Jane on the shoulder. "Are you?"

"Yes, miss," she assured me. "The whole ordeal has been distressing, but I am very glad that you are not worse off. Are you certain we cannot get you anything to help? Are you in any pain?"

I smiled faintly. "I am not. Please do not worry over me unnecessarily. After all, Lucille suffered a worse fate. My father did as well. He might have been dying, but it was murder without a doubt."

The rest of the servants were slowly emerging from their rooms. They spoke in hushed voices and crept through the manor, as if the murderer were still at large. All had been thoroughly searched and questioned, but the detective hadn't revealed more about the situation than necessary. His full report would be given to the Kings.

Williams appeared by Jane's side and placed a heavy hand on her shoulder. "All is taken care of. We will grieve for the tragedies this manor has suffered now, but soon everything will return to its normal workings. We must not validate unfounded rumors throughout the household. It will already be difficult to separate the truth from the lies."

"We will keep it within the family," I agreed.

Williams pursed his lips and then nodded his head once.

Then, I laughed. It was a high-pitched, hysterical sound, and I could hardly believe it left my lips. Jane rose from her seat in a panic, fussing over me, but I waved her away.

"I should have asked you about my family before

this. Should I have, Williams? Do you think it would have saved a life?"

"I would not have told you, Miss Charlotte," he said, his jaw jutting out. "Your father wished to inform you once his will was settled, but as you know, circumstances change. He was right to be afraid of what Victor would do."

"He has done wrong," I said.

"Your father loved your mother dearly, and it was prior to his marriage to Lady Dorothea. Victor was a spoiled child who was unruly. No doubt he was prejudiced toward others."

No matter how often I was told that my father loved my mother, it offered me little comfort. If he had truly loved her, he would not have gone without knowing her whereabouts for so long. It would not have taken him so long for him to find me. I wasn't even sure that he loved me.

I'd never conceived of love as lies and secrets. How could he hide the truth of my parentage and then expect me to take on the responsibilities I'd never seen as my own? How could he leave the estate to me only after Victor had proved himself to be irresponsible? How could I take it on knowing that he'd seen fit to only give me partial truths?

I thought about Williams and how his love for my father blinded him to his master's faults. My father could've believed he was doing the right thing in hiding me from the world, but I didn't agree, and I had to choose whether to accept what he'd left me.

I directed my gaze toward Williams, already knowing the answer before I asked the question. "Did you love my father?"

But instead of answering, Williams teared up and said, "I admired his spirit, as well as your mother's. Nearly as much as I do yours."

"Will you continue to serve this family as loyally as you have in the past? For me?"

He bowed. "Unquestionably, Miss Charlotte."

I chewed on my lip. "I wish I would have known my mother, but I will take on the responsibility of this manor nonetheless."

Williams looked abashed at my pronouncement. He'd played his part in keeping the secret from me as much as my father. "There are, I believe, one or two little portraits of her that your father kept to himself. I will see if I can locate them. And, if you want, miss, I can tell you all I remember of her."

I stood, rested a hand on Williams's shoulder for a brief moment, and said, "I would like that very much. But for now, I would like to be alone."

The servants' voices broke out, rising and lowering in a flurry of questions and statements. I observed some objecting to the questions being posed. Others wanted to know what had really happened. Williams opened his mouth to take charge, but I beat him to it.

"Your questions will be answered in time. For now,

all you need to know is that Mr. van Kirk has passed. Lucille is dead by Victor's hands, and he will not return. I am and have always been the rightful heir to Ivywood Manor. If you wish to contest it, you are free to leave. If you wish to stay, I will keep no secrets from you. Your loyalty to this family will be appreciated and rewarded. This manor will operate differently soon, and I am open to any suggestions you have. But I will not hear them until tomorrow when we are all fed and well rested."

I expected their voices to rise again, but all lapsed into silence. I made my way slowly up the stairs to my bedroom, closed the door, and went to sleep.

THE SOUND, THAT *CLOP, CLOP, CLOP* OF HOOVES ON PATHS, WAS FAMILIAR. THEY MADE SOFT AND SWIFT U-SHAPED INDENTS IN THE GRASS, dusty imprints in the dirt. Willow's muscles were flecked with dirt instead of mud. The lightest sweeping of trousers against it made my riding habit browner and, I thought, me as well.

Mr. van Kirk had prepared Victor for the task of running the manor, and fortunately I'd paid enough attention to understand the goings-on. I still felt uneasy at times. It fell to me to urge Mrs. van Kirk to attend meetings with Jones about the family's affairs with me. She remained in shock from seeing the doctor identify the marks of strangulation on my neck, and she could hardly look at me. Even so, I felt it was necessary for her to stay informed.

The servants reported to me now, and I had listened to many of their suggestions about improving the manor. I had taken up the task of redecorating rooms, adding more plants and color to create a livelier air. On mornings when I was otherwise unoccupied, I rode around the estate. I didn't often ride into town, because word had spread of the deaths that had occurred at Ivywood Manor.

More often than not, the townspeople said our family was cursed. How else could it be that we gained a blushing bride, killed her, and lost our patriarch within the short span of a few months? They greeted me as Miss Herring, but the rumor had spread about which family I truly belonged to.

Mrs. van Kirk wasn't accustomed to my heritage being known, of course, but she quickly came to the conclusion that she was no longer in a position to question me. Her word no longer went very far, as I was privy to every occasion when she requested certain foods or movement of furniture. I made all the final decisions in the household when it came to meals, décor, finances, and everything else.

As a result, she had taken to speaking to me in terse tones in public and formed sentences with the fewest number of words required to convey her messages. I reminded her once when she commented upon the state of our household that it was her son who had put us in this position, and if she did not like it, she was more than welcome to return to her own family. While she was clearly unhappy, she never contradicted my word after that.

Williams claimed that Mrs. van Kirk's attitude stemmed from the fact that she'd loved Mr. van Kirk, even if he hadn't loved her, and it hurt her pride to know otherwise. Theirs was a marriage of convenience, which had undergone careful nurturing under the watchful eyes of their own parents. They'd learned to be happy in their own way. Contrarily, I often thought that Mrs. van Kirk greatly regretted the union.

After an extensive search of the manor, Williams found a few studio portraits of my mother located in my father's old valise. In one, she wore a gown with a square neckline, and her hair was fashioned in a complicated updo. Her face was serious, unsmiling, so unlike the descriptions that I had been given by others. The others had a similar weightiness. Yet her eyes were piercing in all of them.

I laid them out in a half circle around me while I read and reread his travel diaries, particularly the India volume. I memorized every detail until I could merge my parents' story with my own. And I kept the images between the pages of Mr. van Kirk's travel diaries in my bedroom.

I wanted to preserve them, but I also thought that my parents should be together in whatever way this hard world allowed.

"Do you think here might be an ideal spot?" Williams asked.

Williams and I were kneeling on the ground on the south side of the manor. I'd tasked him with holding the gardening hoe while I held one of two pots containing blossoming *Abutilon striatum*. We were loosening the soil with our free hands around the area where I intended to plant the parlor maple. In my haste to rub my cheek, I'd gotten a spot of dirt on me.

I was going to plant flowers for Lucille, and Williams had volunteered to assist me. Together, we watered the bottom of the planting hole, preparing the soil for the roots. We transplanted the parlor maple, ensuring the top of the root ball was even with the ground.

"Will these grow outdoors?" he asked.

I began packing the dirt to rid of air pockets around the plant. "They'll thrive."

Williams stared at the soil spotting my garments and skin. He said Jane would have a fit about washing them again. At least she was forced to clean trousers instead of gowns now that I had so much freedom.

I made a *tch* sound in the back of my throat. "Trousers withstand much more than my gowns ever did. Besides, planting these flowers is my only concern."

I gave the soil another pat, and Williams helped even out the surrounding area. I handed him the flowerless pot while I wiped my hands clean against my trousers. He shook his head at me ever so slightly.

"It looks uneven there," I commented, though Williams took no real offense.

"You would think I'd never transplanted flowers before."

I straightened and placed my hands on my hips. "You said you did not possess much talent in gardening, and I was inclined to believe you. How can I trust you with transplanting if you tell me things like that?"

He seemed thoughtful. "I do not know, Miss Charlotte."

Williams rose and offered his arm to me. We stepped back to admire our handiwork. I was anxious to see them do well, though I'd never transplanted this particular species.

"You shall help me care for it?" I asked.

His eyes softened. "Of course."

"Do you think Lucille would have liked them? She was never interested in gardening herself."

"She enjoyed looking at them though."

"That is true. Shall we plant my mother's?"

I picked up the second pot of *Abutilon striatum* and held it out to Williams. He took the flowers gingerly, and I worked on digging the hole this time. When we were done planting the last of the flowers, Williams looked relieved.

"Now, we can return indoors, so that Jane may fuss over you properly."

I grinned. "I do believe I will let her this time."

Author's Acknowledgments

I am grateful to my parents, Garry and Sherrie, for their unwavering love and support. Thank you to my friends for their endless conversation and food.

Thank you to the English Department and Honors Program at the University of Hawaiʻi at Mānoa, where this project began. Professor Shawna Yang Ryan guided me throughout the writing process and commented on numerous revisions. Dr. Anna Feuerstein aided me in my research of the late Victorian era.

Finally, without the team at Brain Mill Press, especially Ruth Homrighaus and Mary Ann Hudson, this novella would not have come to fruition. Thank you for embracing Charlotte's story.

About the Author

Tani Loo was born and raised in Honolulu, Hawai'i. Her work has appeared in publications such as *Hawaii Review* and *Honolulu Civil Beat*.

About the Cover Artist

Rovina Cai is a freelance illustrator based in Melbourne, Australia. She works out of an old convent building that is possibly haunted. Her work has been recognized by the Society of Illustrators and the Children's Book Council of Australia. Recently, she has illustrated books by Patrick Ness and Margo Lanagan.

9 781948 559416